WITHIN AND BEYOND
THE REALMS OF THE SUN
by
Bruce S. Larson

WITHIN AND BEYOND: THE REALMS OF THE SUN
by
Bruce S. Larson

Published by
World Line One Press

ISBN: 978-0-9856841-2-9

Cover art, and all images © Bruce S. Larson.

For my Mother, Gladys, who taught me to appreciate the words of others while encouraging me to create worlds of my own.

CONTENTS

ACKNOWLEDGEMENTS

My sincere thanks to Bonnie Hammond for her excellent and indispensable work on this volume's cover. Her contribution makes this book ride tall on the shelf.

I again express my thanks to Erik England for his invaluable work on the cover background art. Here's to another successful ascent, above and beyond.

I want to acknowledge the consideration and support of my colleagues Cristopher DeRose and Michael McCarty. Find their considerable works wherever quality fiction is sold.

I am grateful for the support found each Second Thursday, and from all friends and family throughout the year. Art is life. Thank you, one and all.

And cheers to you who bought or borrowed this book. Thank you.

PREFACE

The tale "Southern Sun" inspired this book's title. *Millennium SF&F* first published it in both their online and print editions. It also has a home on my website. I place it here as an extra story (or "bonus track"), and lead off for the other tales. It also serves as a salute to the past, and all who continue the journey today. Writing can be a hard trek, but also a rewarding and hopefully long adventure.

In my earliest of early days as a writer, I submitted a story I considered Fantasy. I was soon schooled otherwise. A letter written in direct response to my submission (a rarity then and now) informed me that my use of language meant my story must be Science Fiction because it lacked the right phrasing to be considered Fantasy. Therefore, elements such as Setting, Theme, and perhaps the presence of a sword did not place it within the genre where I thought it belonged. This was also a valuable lesson in targeting markets with the right piece. (Although, that remains as much a practical art as magic without any hint of science, fictional or otherwise.) I remain grateful for that personal response and all others from considerate editors. Time moves on. I like to think my use of language has improved, even if it never adopted a particular manner for a specific market. Now, you read my latest collection to date. Allow me a personal response of "thank you" for choosing this book, and for actually reading the Preface.

You will notice I dare apply the term Fantasy to this book, as well as Science Fiction. I didn't write these stories using a filter or blender (word processing program, yes). The stories are combinations of those genres, and perhaps others. (Speculative Fiction, anyone?) Combination happens in real life as well as imagination. A prism in the path of white light reveals a rainbow spectrum. Each of the spectrum's colors can mix into many vivid hues. Isaac Newton created a spectrum of seven main colors corresponding to the seven notes on the musical scale. (How is that for combining ideas from separate fields?) If you place your mind in the path of a sentence, the words become a spectrum of thought. Words weave spells, describe equations, and open portals to other worlds. All such experiences can occur within a single story. There are several stories here, all awaiting a willing mind. It will be a fun ride. As you read, each realm will become real, at least for a time. Time now to start the first journey.

Bruce S. Larson
Somewhere on Earth (or so it seems), 2013

SOUTHERN SUN

Connor sat on the cooling grass with legs folded. The southern traveling sun had just set completely. Its western roaming sibling had dropped below the edge of the plateau, but was still sinking into the true horizon beyond. Its light reflected across the wasteland surrounding the plateau, tarnishing the sky dusky bronze. Most people were in their homes now. The domestic noises mingled with the sound of the wind across the plateau's jagged sides. Connor's people had created a small world close to the clouds. Their immigrant culture fused tradition with the abandoned artifacts and housing they found after completing the treacherous and deadly climb up. A long falling trickle of water spurred their desperate ascent. Connor made the climb when very little. Then, dream images of sleep and awake were the land and water high above. Now, Connor looked out across the path of the southern sun, and wondered what new dawn it made in lands below and far away.

Before the upheavals, this shard of civilization once connected to the rest of the world. Crumbled streets ended at the sharp edges of the plateau. The surrounding land below became an expanding waste. On top became a near paradise with hard work. It was peaceful. It was prison if your imagination strayed over the distant, true horizon. Few boundaries restrained the dreams of the strong of limb and mind. Connor was now strong enough to carry the family sword. By now, Father had taught his eager offspring all he could. Connor knew this. The lessons had grown shorter, repetitive, and farther between.

Connor drew the sword and brandished it to the sky. The blade reflected the evening light. Its length looked like the wings of the giant pterodons flying in the intense bright of midday. Typically then, people stayed inside from the heat and fear that the high soaring beasts would find them easy prey. However, Connor watched the sky giants soar south. Singular

1

purpose seemed to propel them. Or perhaps the pterodons were guided.

The southern sun over the outstretched wings made their skin translucent yellow. Western light cast faint, fleeting shadows across their underbellies as that sun hinted at descent. Connor was certain harnesses crisscrossed the sleek, avian breasts. Such rigging would have to be vast, and require industry. Industry on the plateau was small, but plateau culture manufactured constraints of its own.

Suddenly the earth shook. The ground cracked deep and sundered into smaller masses along the widening crevasse. Heat and the scent of burning soil singed Connor's nostrils as rocks burst skyward like volcanic missiles.

Another upheaval? No!

The deep and savage cry betrayed the monster before it burst through the convulsing surface. It glared down at Connor as rubble cascaded from its massive, scaly shoulders. It opened its hideous, crocodilian mouth and roared again. Flames spewed forth and seared the earth as if cast from both suns. Connor tumbled aside. The ground burned to glass from the creature's assault. Connor leapt to the beast's chest, and quickly ascended the razor surface. Connor's hands bled, but the beast must never get the chance to burn and rampage to the city's heart.

Massive claws swiped at Connor as the sword slashed deeply between wide, emerald scales. Thick, acrid blood flowed out like magma. The monster motioned to scream, but Connor's further slashes denied even sound from its savaged throat. The beast fell. Connor leapt from its plummeting body. There was no sound as Connor saw the house collapse under the monster's dead mass. There was no cheering. The monster faded as the daydream ended. If the monster had been real and not imaginary, only the few people of the plateau would have sung Connor praises. No other peoples would ever hear of the epic deed.

Connor glanced at the doorway. The youngest of the family, brother Wil, had watched the sword flash in Connor's hands. Wil smiled from the opened door. Connor slid the sword back into the scabbard and smiled back at Wil, and then looked back to the setting point of the south wandering sun. Social barriers held back Connor's dreams of wandering. In a vanished age, people were rooted everywhere. Then the upheavals shattered the landscape, and migration became survival. Connor was born into that age. Static life on the plateau rebuilt those unseen barriers. People reinforced them with courtly smiles and knowing glances. Those expressions were surface reflections of deeper expectations. Connor saw these expressions also cast at Victor who lived nearby. Victor's duty to his family was expected to be clear. Perhaps those social structures would grow stronger, just as the plateau's land flourished anew.

Connor looked again into the house. Family members darted past the doorway. There was enough food, and enough hands to collect it. With five, children were of no shortage to Connor's parents. The family would be deprived of only the razor edged heirloom, now rightfully Connor's. The stars began to dominate the sky, taking over from the reluctant western sun finally submerged under the horizon. Soon sleep would call. Connor resolved to make both the dreams of sleep and awake a reality. New images would fill the searching mind. Perhaps even stranger ones than fiery beasts erupting from the ground.

The next afternoon, when the suns were ebbing, Victor watched his fated love leave for an uncertain destiny. Proximity atop the plateau predetermined the beautiful young Connor would be his wife. There were few other women to know, let alone love. Now, that fate grew less certain was with each of Connor's steps to the plateau's edge. Victor was certain Connor could make the climb down. There would certainly be no stopping her. Victor, however, had his brothers to raise. Yet, once that was a mother's task. He began to look to the southern sun, and wondered. Should he go after her? Connor left few others to take her place, be they beautiful or otherwise. Later, Victor would dream of his own path under the arc of the pterodons, pursuing his own desire. Connor herself became the stuff of dreams.

ENCHANTMENT

The bed was warm. Cozy. Still, a cool sensation against Jerry's face woke him. It was drool. While asleep, his open mouth had created a dreaded damp spot on the giant, shared pillow Dara had bought for their bed. The worst was yet to come. The rhythm of their sleep meant that Jerry should turn and face Dara, and she would slink closer to him. It wasn't the potent, minty fresh assault of her enchanted toothpaste that he dreaded. It was her face sliding over the pillow and hitting the damp spot. A rudely awakened Dara was worse than a dozen cursed emails accidentally opened at work and the MT troll glaring at him with those huge and malignant yellow eyes. Well, Jerry thought, an annoyed Dara was not that bad, but was not something he enjoyed. However, if he just stayed parked on the mattress, then their broken pattern would wake her for sure. He was doomed.

Jerry strained to raise his neck and peer across the darkened bedroom. Even in the dim light he could see the moving patterns on the charmed pillow case. It was a sea motif. Jerry frowned. Still, Dara's penchant for enchanted merchandise meant there were a lot of magic applications on her phone. One made spilled drinks vanish. That should also work for pillow drool. He reached for her phone and smiled as his fingers silently lifted it off the nightstand.

"Did you drool, again?"

Dara's sudden question spooked Jerry more than if their shrieking loon fire alarm had sounded. Dara's phone shot from his fingers and hit Dara's dressing chair. The phone's operating fairy materialized in its nimbus as the small, slim machine teetered on the chair arm. The fairy shot Jerry a fleeting glare as the phone fell to the carpet. Jerry thought the fairy was creepier than it should be. It appeared more like an annoyed dragon fly than a tiny, flying girl.

"Um," was Jerry's tactfully evasive reply. He could see the fairy's pulsing glow from it whirling around the phone

5

below the edge of the bed. He knew there was no danger of stepping on it. Dara had a motile phone that would crawl back to its last location via Magical Positioning System.

"You did." Dara said.

Jerry could feel more than see Dara's eyes shoot open and stare at him.

"Uh, yeah."

"Aura." Dara said. It was a single word spell to make the bedroom paint become luminous.

"Sorry, sweetheart." Jerry hoped his words would brighten Dara's attitude.

"First, you didn't call the pest control guys like I asked." Dara pushed herself to a sitting position. "Now you drench my pillow!"

"Drench?" Jerry did a one shoulder shrug while lying on his side. "Well, maybe. Pest guys? No."

Dara squinted and began to formulate more complaints, but Jerry spoke first.

"Besides. Don't you have an app for that?"

"No." Dara folded her arms. "You need a professional Caster to get rid of that thing crawling around outside. I think it calls for a counter-creature to drive it off. You need someone with all the permits."

Jerry grunted. The sound reminded Dara of the thing skulking outside that she wanted removed.

"It showed up after the new mattress came." Dara said. "The delivery guy probably left it after you shorted him on the tip."

"So I need to pay a service guy a fee for a curse left by another service guy?" Jerry rubbed his eyes adjusting to the light.

"Something like that." Dara snarled. "Stop being cheap."

"Cheap? What am I a billionaire?" Jerry leaned up and waved his free arm. "Get me an app that makes money from air."

6

Dara leaned over and plucked her phone from its ascent of the nightstand. The fairy dove within the phone to assist her searching. For a seemingly long, arduous moment, the only sound was Dara's fingers against the small plastic screen.

Jerry answered Dara's silence. "All it does is crawl around outside. Outside!"

"And make shadows through the windows," Dara said still focused on her phone. "And some sound like a goat farting."

"Then just be glad it's only an audio-visual curse." Jerry laughed to himself.

Dara was silent, again.

"Look," Jerry slowly inhaled. "I'll call the delivery guys' boss. If he sent it, then he'll get rid of it."

"Maybe he'll just escalate with a stronger curse!"

"Trust me," Jerry eased back to the mattress. "Atonement is easier to take than unemployment. He'll do it. By tomorrow, no more shadows. Or goat noises."

"Drool?" Dara looked down harshly at Jerry.

"Yeah. And powerful, minty freshness."

Dara raised her eyebrows.

Jerry smiled. He lifted his hand and very softly caressed the edge of her chin and enjoyed gazing at her face. Dara's expression was still lit by aggravation as Jerry slid down and closed his eyes. He was still smiling.

Dara placed her phone over the pillow. The fairy darted out and the moist patch near Jerry's ear disappeared into a cloud resembling a flower. Jerry scratched his ear lobe without opening his eyes. Dara liked to see magic work. She thought of several mornings when the pull strings on Jerry's hooded sweater dipped into his coffee when he leaned over the table. When he sat back, brown drops would flick out of his mug and fly across the clean table cloth. Dara enjoyed seeing the little brown dots vanish as different colored puffs when the ever-white spell did its work. She had bought the table cloth, and Jerry's sweater.

Dara looked at her phone screen, and then glanced back at Jerry. Her expression softened. She would let Jerry expel the odd thing outside. She clicked off the fairy and its extranet search efforts. The main screen appeared. There were plenty of icons to summon information and dispel annoyances. No software app or beneficial spell taught how to love and tolerate someone. They weren't the same thing, but she had found that emotional alchemy with Jerry. That was no magic spell, but it was enchantment. Somehow this stingy, occasionally aggravating drooler had captivated her heart through persistence and personal charm.

"Peace," Dara said.

The walls dimmed. Dara turned off her phone and put it aside. She leaned down and kissed Jerry's dry cheek. Dara curled next to him and pulled the blankets over both of them. They both smiled under the covers.

THE AFAR

The white sun shone brightly in the light azure sky. The day moon chased it as it rose towards noon. Cleave hawks circled high near the edges of a sun ring. Eyna ran out beneath them, more frightened by what lay behind him. It was Testing Time. All the children of his age were gathered in the polis hall where Administrators and Mages gave tests to guide the near adults toward careers and better habits. Eyna didn't want direction, especially from strangers with pointed questions and condescending stares. He did not do well on directed paths. Eyna studied, but not always the assigned subjects. He loved to learn about living things on this enchanted planet. He doubted the inquisitors knew as much about this world as he did. But you couldn't ask questions, only answer them. Eyna felt life grew beyond controls. He defied the inquisition and its expectations. He would find his own way. His mother often said that if he stayed so headstrong he would grow up to be a bull. That felt a better option, today. Eyna sprinted from the outlaying farm building across a fallow pasture. Cheer weeds squealed as his feet hit them and their seeds leapt into the air. Eyna ran faster. The forest stood beyond the pasture. Freedom lay beyond it. Or at least better places to hide. Eyna bounded over the fence and into the wet, mossy rain forest. Immediately he discovered where his boots leaked. He pressed forward. His breaths now felt cold and wet. It was early Spring, and rain season was just ebbing. On his world, Sauris, magic and a nature wed to raise several distinct ecologies. Some were very dangerous. All were wondrous. Beyond the forest was the most awe striking life on any world, anywhere.

Eyna charged through saplings, low branches, dangling moss and underbrush. Twigs and branches snapped. He stopped, and tore moss from his face. He was making too much noise. Eyna also realized the forest would not appreciate him forcing his way through with such spite. He slowed and began ducking through the branches and weaving around the thickest

9

brush. He paused to listen for the approach of people in pursuit. There was none. Maybe they only shrugged when he bolted, or were unable to give chase with old limbs and lungs. Perhaps they thought his defiance could never propel him outside the city reach. He would prove them wrong. He thought he might one day return to the polis to see his family, after his triumph and adventure. He continued deeper into the forest, quietly and respectfully. The babble of a swift stream greeted him. He stepped out from a cluster of tall ruby ferns onto its bank. His quiet approach allowed him to behold a gift or perhaps receive judgment. Eyna's eyes widened.

At this time of year, most humans were yet to venture back into the wilderness. Perhaps that is why a Rue was so close to the polis. They were shorter than humans, but about as round in the center as a man who rarely ventured beyond a chair. Unlike most of those humans, Rues had muscular shoulders. Like a lot of those men, Rues had fury faces that no razor could cleave, but also fury bodies. They stood on two legs, but could amble well on all fours. Their name came from the way they always looked back over their shoulders with a rueful look. They stayed away from humans as if out of scorn for settling their planet generations ago. Even today, people knew little about Rue lives, or Rue culture. Some said that if humanity had never set forth on Sauris, then the Rues would be its dominant intelligent life. People told stories of small Rue villages in glades within deep woods. Eyna had never seen one. He recalled drawings of Rues wearing satchels and belts. Still, Eyna doubted Rues were anything more advanced than the extinct raccoon. Then the Rue turned to him. Eyna could clearly see the sack of woven grass tied into strands of long fur on its left side, and the ornate walking stick just long enough for a Rue hand to grasp. Eyna became rapt by its knowing, and yes, regretful stare from its triangular face. It left along the stream banks to the west. Eyna shuddered. It was at times frightening to feel the stare of a wild creature in its home. It was near awe when it looked back with intelligence, and perhaps accusation.

Eyna trekked more slowly eastward along the banks. He came to a bend in the stream. A recent surge had cut a steep bank on the opposite shore. The exposed soil was now a muddy slope. The smell of composting forest floor and muck was pungent. Mussels slowly scaled the glistening bank, half submerged in mud. Their single, top shells were a mostly flat teardrop shape. They were almost impossible to pry off rocks or hardened sandbars. Found like this in soft mud, it would be a feast in some home. Neighbors would be invited. Some inns let patrons keep the shells. Nice, unchipped shells hung along their rafters over tables. Mussel shells were mostly shades of grey. Some sported a few bands of black. Fewer still had lines of white. The one time Eyna and his family ate mussel at an inn was one of his cherished memories. Later he learned the cooked meat was the creature's large, single foot. He sneered at the thought of eating anything's feet, and now he saw wild mussels with his own eyes. More importantly, he smelled where they lived with his own nose. Eyna wondered who would capture and cook a creature that lived in wet, smelly mud. If he had been hungry, the sensation vanished. He rubbed his gut and imagined his face must look a lot like a Rue.

Eyna found a fallen evergreen that lay across the stream and at a slight angle over the forest floor beyond. He hopped onto it and headed south towards living things that inspired awe, not stomach aches. He made good time along the elevated trail of bark and vertical branches. His only impedance was the few thick limbs in the center of his path. He gripped the limbs tightly when he swung around them so he wouldn't slip and plummet into the dense undergrowth below the trunk. A slapping noise echoed ahead where the foliage appeared to fall away. Eyna's raised trail served as a bridge again. The fallen tree took him over a shallow pond. Ripples flowed from the far bank from behind a whorl of pepper berry stalks. The stalks were thick with leaves, but had yet to blossom. They were weeks away from offering their spicy fruit. Behind them, something worked to make the slapping noise.

A rainbow captivated Eyna. Sunbeams lanced through mossy filaments dangled from an alder tree on the far bank. The rainbow flared within the tendrils. The spectral bands broke into angular sections within the chaotic web. Glistening drops tantalized among the colors. Eyna could smell their sweetness drifting over to him. It appeared that the weight of the drops might snap the web. Eyna mused that if the moss broke, the rainbow would escape. However, he focused on liberating some of the drops. He climbed out as far as he dared along a thick branch. A sudden swarm of angel wasps darted out and flew back and forth over the water. Their rapid wing beats made a weird vibration inside his ears when they darted by his head. He slid back towards the trunk. The angel wasps sped back into the forest and avoided the rainbow. As Eyna's feet met the safety of the trunk, he rubbed his ears. The thing making the slapping noise moved beyond the pepper berry. Eyna gripped the tree bark.

The mud bug's legs ended in sword points that stabbed deeply into the soft brown edges of the pond. Although the creature did live in mud, it was one hundred times the size of anything threatened by a boot heel. The thing was deep maroon in color with a glint like wet steel. Eyna doubted anything made from real steal could pierce its heavy shell. Any weapon would probably get snapped apart by its two massive foreclaws. The claws appeared almost as scythes hinged atop great drops of molten iron, now cooled and hard. Its eyes sat jabbed on long stalks that swept forward from its blunt rear end. Eyna remembered diagrams of these monsters in illumina at the library. The body in three dimensions looked akin to a huge, squashed helmet. He knew the 'eyes' were truly more for sensing odors than light. The odors of mud were important. It ate it. The mud bug quickly gathered up a huge glob. Two curved plates opened at its front. Behind these plates swept one million sifting fingers. Its mouth lay somewhere beyond them.

12

The glob tumbled through its mouth and fell back to the claws as a perfect sphere. The mud bug tossed the sphere aside and gathered another glob. The sphere immediately began to melt back into the bank. Although Eyna thought the mud bug was truly weird, its precise movements and the perfection of its temporary spheres captivated him.

Mud bugs were yet another creature that ate smelly muck. No one ate mud bugs, though. Eyna understood why forest hunters only pried the mussels out of streams. No one would attack what could so obviously fight back. It noticed him. The claws raised and opened. Eyna knew this was a threat display. It began to move back to the pepper berries. Passed them was Eyna on his tree. He resolved not to test a mud bug's ability to climb a fallen trunk. Eyna moved quickly, again. He pressed on with no one or no thing chasing him. The fallen tree began to narrow. Eyna was reaching the end of his overground trail. If he had traveled up the tree when it was standing, he would be high enough to see across the forest and back to the polis. Still he would not be as high from the ground as the tops of what he hoped to see within minutes. The fallen tree had cleaved an opening at the edge of the forest that the fast growing plants had yet to close. Sunlight shone brightly from the open expanse beyond. At the forest edge, the trunk was no wider than a thick branch, and there many more small limbs filled with evergreen needles. Eyna vaulted over as many as he could. The angle of most towards the end meant diving below them and pushing through walls of needles. Their sting was not as much a concern as the fear he might meet another creature with great claws or accusing eyes in the shadows. His feet finally reached the end. He bid the guiding tree good bye and charged into sunlight.

Eyna stopped inches short of plunging to his death. Kicked rocks rolled before his boots and plunged over the edge of the cliff. Eyna blinked as his eyes adjusted to the light. It took human eyes a little longer to do this in the clear light of the Saurisan sun. Beyond the cliff was Crater Valley. These craters were as not caused by titanic impacts, but by titanic things leaving the planet. They were things beyond physics and reason. Yet, they were a fact of life on Sauris, and how Sauris spread life to other worlds. Eyna was finally where they grew. He was almost fearful of looking over at them farther off in the valley. They stood impossibly still, as if in a frame of time all their own. They were majestic and the apex of life evolving within the environment of magic. They were the legendary giant mushrooms.

They grew in towering groups called troops or clutches. No bridges were allowed to span from the cliffs to the tops of the mushrooms. The mushrooms would grow taller and stretch the bridges, anyway. Their height would surpass the high cliffs and thoughts that such a living things could not exist. Eyna was already tired from his forest trek. No matter. With the giants in sight, his journey had just started. They were still a long hike away, unless he had a rope or wings. He had neither. Even if a trader happened by, he would first ask for dry socks. To reach the giants, Eyna would need to skirt the cliff and break cover along the steep road heading into the valley. After a sprint along the cliffs, Eyna slid and tumbled down the rough roadside. Dust made him cough and clung to his sweaty skin. He has happy. Inside Crater Valley he could enter the base of the clutch. He left the road and made his own trail across the grassland that covered the valley. It was a line of sight charge to the epic things that drew him here with the hopes of great adventure.

Each clutch was a world unto itself. A guardian called a Tender watched over a clutch that showed the potential to reach epic size. This person protected against disease, disaster, and human exploitation. At least they did as best they could. Most poleis thought the magic life of the clutch was worth protecting. Still, the tender was a typical solitary figure with an entire realm to patrol. Depending on the Tender's personality, they could act as a hermit, tour guide, or stern sheriff. Most folk respected them. For, in the end, the responsibility meant self-sacrifice not just of time and effort, but of life. At least the Tender's life on Sauris. The same power that granted the epic size to the clutch would eventually take it. The clutch of titanic mushrooms and all life they held would tear from the surface in an event that would mark a single epoch on most other worlds. The clutch would soar aloft and ever upward beyond the airs of Sauris and into the Afar. The Tender also sailed off with the small world, and was never seen again. All, expect one. Tender Jono Evandon came back from the Afar. He was legend. And legend said this was his clutch.

In springtime, the shadow of this clutch would span for miles to the north. Of course, Eyna was approaching from the south. The sun felt hot on his neck. Eyna wished the streams of the forest magically flowed before him, now. The dew still clinging to the thicker grass slaked his thirst a little bit. Desire to finish his trek powered him onward. Eyna was sure the clutch would hold life more amazing than the forest. Perhaps there was so much life inside mushrooms that even the Tender couldn't know it all. Once he began to explore it, Eyna hoped to find a unique creature or plant never seen before his eyes came across it. He also hoped it would be something easily caught or picked and safe to eat. He was hungry. Another sensation gripped him. He felt as if struck by a strong wind that never blew passed him, and an odd buzzing coursed though his body without sound. Eyna looked up. He was nearing the outer edge of the great saucer like caps extending out from the massive stems. The cap's gills were so high that soaring birds flew beneath them. Eyna felt the force that supported the mushrooms and connected them to worlds beyond. He never expected it to be a strong, physical sensation. He paused and reconsidered his next step. He had never been in the presence of something so huge and alive. He moved his boot forward and kept hiking on toward the clutch.

The grassland stopped as the ground rose at the base of the closest mushroom. Small crystals lay mixed with the bare earth. Eyna ascended the rise without thought of celebration.

The success of his journey came to him suddenly when he rested against the vast mushroom stem. He felt an extra crackle of their energy. He slid his hand across the stem. It was impossibly smooth for the skin of something so thick. He could still feel more than see vertical strands akin to twine fibers or the ridges of a mussel shell. Eyna smiled. The spaces between the mushrooms made an arcing trailway deeper into the clutch. Eyna hopped onto an opposite arc so he wouldn't stumble back out into the grassland. It grew cooler. Eyna discovered his sweaty clothes and layer of road dirt were not very insulating. There was still light. The mushrooms glowed. On dark, cloudy nights, gentle light from clutches reflected off the cloud canopy and was visible from miles away. Eyna walked onward.

Something else walked in the arcing trails. Eyna heard a sound as if many, heavy fingers drummed against the ground. The drummer was big. It must have as many legs as a pentapede, or be one of many. Eyna felt chased, again. He wanted to find an arc back to the grassland, as anything that hunted within the stems probably didn't want to be exposed. But he had come too far inside the clutch. Eyna found himself racing into a small glen among the stems. At its center grew brilliant flowers as tall as people. They wafted in a breeze he couldn't feel. The drumming grew louder. His pursuer was just behind him. He braced himself against a mushroom to face it, or them. His heart raced faster than ever as the giant spiders flowed into the glen.

Each of the arachnids was the same shade of grey as the interior mushrooms. The spiders were oddly fleshy. Eyna thought there must be at least a hundred of them, and all of them huge. They sprinted towards Eyna. He instinctively curled into ball. The spiders raced over him and up the stem. Through his fingers gripping his head, he saw their undersides and legs running over him as they bumped him side to side. The last spider ran over Eyna. He looked up along its path. A man stood on the side of the stem as a living shelf. The spiders ran around him. The man reached down to stroke a spider's back as it raced passed him. Even from distance, Eyna could see the man's piercing blue eyes. The sapphire stare focused on Eyna, and he wondered if he would have fared better if eaten by the spiders. The man walked down the mushroom at a right angle to Eyna, whose boots trembled against the flat ground. The impossible man's feet adhered to the mushroom's surface as if he was a spider himself. He wore heavy pants and a worn jacket. A satchel and several smaller pouches hung down towards the earth. His pockets appeared ironically flat and empty. He stopped just above Eyna's head, still staring.

"I am Jono Evandon, and you are a trespasser."

Eyna stood gaping at Jono. To him, this white haired man with burning blue eyes seemed to be an absolute ruler with no patience for transgression. Jono sighed. He flexed his shoulders as he raised his chin to glance at the flowers. He returned his gaze back to Eyna, but with a focus less like a spear.

"And, you are likely thirsty and tired." Jono said. He dropped a pouch to Eyna. "You can eat and drink that, but not here. The flowers make my nose itch."

Eyna held the pouch but wondered how he could join Jono on the stem. Jono leapt down beside Eyna. Jono led Eyna to a grotto where the space between stems was wide enough for a perceptible breeze, but no flowers to offended Jono's nose. They sat on a surprisingly warm boulder to enjoy the view. Opposite them, a stream flowed around a mushroom to create a curling waterfall. Eyna had no idea what filled the sandwich he ate, or how Jono made bread. Still, it was tasty enough, and Eyna didn't want to offend the man that he originally thought might eat him.

"Am I the first?" Eyna's full stomach restored his courage.

"The first what?" Jono asked.

"To make it here."

"No." Jono shook his head. "I've been here quite a long while."

"But—"

"And, of course, no other young nip from a polis has ever tried to run away and venture to a clutch. It's unheard of." Jono smiled at Eyna. "Still, I suppose you should be complimented on your perseverance to get this far." Jono looked away from Eyna, but still smiled.

For an instant, Eyna felt he could smile.

"But you won't be." Jono said.

Eyna frowned.

Jono withdrew a set of field glasses from his satchel and handed them to Eyna.

"There." Jono pointed high up the stem above the curling waterfall.

Eyna quickly scanned with the glasses to find Jono's target.

"Look for the green patch on high just below the shadow of the cap." Jono said. "It's where the sun gets through, and the alga grows on the stems."

Eyna found the patch of green.

"You see them?" Jono asked.

"Yes!" Eyna chirped. "The spiders!"

A group of the same grey beasts that raced over Eyna gathered at the edge of the vertical alga field. Jono tapped the glasses and Eyna could seem them with greater magnification. The spiders used spade like fangs to scrape the flat vegetation off the mushroom without harming its surface.

"Over many generations, the original arachnids grew and adapted with the influence of the clutches." Jono said. "Once they ate other bugs, now they eat like cows."

"What's a cow?" Eyna asked.

"A big mammal that eats like a spider." Jono answered.

"I'm not sure they could ever eat a mud bug," Eyna handed the glasses back to Jono.

"Probably not." Jono said, and replaced his field glasses inside the satchel. "But as there are many different things on

Sauris than on other worlds, things are even more different within the clutch. For one thing, no mud bugs."

"I was sure of it. The differences of life. It's was why I came here. To see the creatures." Eyna gushed with enthusiasm. He then winced at recalling that his first encounter with clutch life had not gone well.

"You didn't run here to be a Tender?" Jono asked.

"No. I came here to find new creatures. Maybe one even you haven't seen."

"Good luck with that." Jono smiled.

"Do you go up as high as the spiders?" Eyna asked.

"Yes."

"Could I go there?" Eyna asked almost crouching to a kneeling position.

Another focused stare was Jono's reply. Eyna's heart sank, but Jono's following remark gave it a boost.

"It's where I was going before you appeared."

"I could help!" Eyna bolted to standing.

"Probably not." Jono said. "Still, it might save me time. It was my one chore before company comes. Expected company."

"You get visitors?" Eyna asked.

"Of every sort you could imagine. And many more you cannot. I suppose I have some responsibility to you now, unless I let an adder or a wolf take you." Jono sighed.

"What's a wolf?" Eyna raised his eyebrows.

"An amphibian that carries its young on its back, but can still kill a mud bug and eat you at the same time." Jono answered.

"And they come in here?"

"Frequently."

Jono left Eyna in the grotto. He assured Eyna that no wolves would come hunting today. It was Thursday. Eyna didn't understand, but stayed put. When Jono returned he slung Eyna into a harness that smelled like the bottom of a trunk not opened since before his birth. Eyna said nothing so Jono wouldn't reconsider taking him up the stem. The harness dangled a body length down from Jono. Eyna didn't understand how Jono had the strength to haul him, and Jono's pouches and satchel up the stem even clinging to the mushroom's surface with hands and feet. Eyna wondered if Jono tapped the magic properties of the clutch. He did feel lighter, somehow. He also felt awkward. Eyna thought himself young and strong, but a man with white hair was hauling him like a sack of potatoes. Eyna tried not to squirm as much as the harvested roots typically did.

Eyna noticed they crossed a stretch of lighter color on the ascent. He thought it was where spiders had eaten a patch of algae. He looked over at a pack of spiders on another stem. From here, they seemed more like aphids. An idea struck Eyna: perhaps, given enough time, all life will become all other types of life. Then he thought of his own life, dangling higher up than was possible in any tree. He looked at the great, living columns descending down to the grotto that was now a tiny speck where he once ate a sandwich. He hoped he would not lose that sandwich from his gut. Wind gusts pushed him slightly sideways. Before he would gain greater swing, Jono would reach back and steady the harness. Eyna felt even safer from the occasional, confident wink from Jono.

They neared the apex of the exposed stem below the spanning cap. The stem continued up inside the cap among the dark folds of the gills. The gills were the great partitions of tissue radiating from the stem. Each one stretched to the bottom edge of the circular cap. Eyna saw the actual thickness of the gills that appeared thin from the ground. Here the mushrooms generated, stored, and eventually spewed billions of spores. Their release came as a great cloud leaving the clutch and dispersing across the entire planet. It would be an event carried out on other worlds from clutches like this one having sailed out across space. The people of Sauris knew from Jono's account that the magic of the clutch held its own atmosphere. Most creatures inside it survived the voyage. Eyna wondered if they could survive where they landed out in the Afar. Jono had.

Eyna noticed a swarm of something buzzing between the gills. Perhaps it was a collective hive creature that never left the protection of the cap. The swarm would be massive. The rush of wind made asking question impossible. That, and Eyna didn't want to cause Jono to slip from distraction. Eyna was almost afraid to continue up into the gills and complete darkness. This close, the space between gills straight above was like a titanic mouth threatening to engulf them. The black field extended beyond his field of vision. Eyna's mind tried to align his orientation along the closest gill as if it was the horizon. For a moment, Eyna had the sensation of floating completely free. There was a tug of the harness line. Eyna looked up. Jono mouthed a sentence to Eyna who understood he was trying to ease concerns. But for what? Then Jono left the stem and began crawling like a fly upside down along the edge of the gill. Eyna dangled directly below his back. He worried the sweat from his palms would fall as rain or weaken his harness. Eyna kept looking up. He preferred the darkness between the gills to the plummeting feeling when he looked at the ground. He was utterly unable to affect his fate. At least not in a positive way. His life was now solely in the care of Jono Evandon, and the strength of seemingly ancient rope. Eyna almost screamed when Jono took a hand away from the gill and pointed down. Eyna trembled but glanced passed his dangling feet. Not far below was the sloping cap of a smaller mushroom. Its close surface was a welcome sight. Eyna hoped he would stop trembling by the time he touched its grey, wondrous, and very solid surface.

"You all right, nip?" Jono asked as he freed Eyna from the harness now that they both stood safely on the cap.

"Yes. I—I'm Ennya."

"Ennya? Odd name for a boy."

"I mean Eyna!"

"That's better. So, Eyna, welcome to my garden!"

Jono waved his hand to the healthy garden plot several steps from the cap's edge. The mushroom they walked upon was smaller, but still wide enough to hold a polis' central hub. Most important for the garden, a large area of its cap expanded out beneath open sky.

"This cap gets enough light and rain. I have to bring the dirt, seeds, and tools." Jono said as they reached the garden.

"Do you need to grow this food?"

"Strictly, no. But, even when accustomed to the harvests from the clutch, a person always hankers for what they knew before this life. This is my indulgence." Jono smiled.

Eyna thought of Jono's life. He had known life before becoming a Tender, and then a life out in the Afar. Eyna stared at the garden and wondered if any of these vegetables were from another world. If so, perhaps Eyna could add another chapter to Jono's legend. Eyna watched Jono harvest some carrots from the blackest soil he'd ever seen, but the act was so typical of life anywhere. Jono now seemed so human. Eyna recalled the stories of Jono's travels into the Afar inside his first clutch. Out there he met other travelers: The Tetuarians. They and their metal ship sailed Jono back home to Sauris. There was a statue commemorating the events in the next polis over, Everfield. Eyna's own polis, Alterwood, had no statues, but a better library. Every library on Sauris had several books on Jono Evandon. And now Eyna stood beside him atop a giant mushroom that would one day enter space. He suddenly felt very tired. Jono handed Eyna a carrot. Eyna was lost to his thoughts and bit into it without brushing off the last bits of dirt.

Dinner was a salad picked hand to mouth. Jono and Eyna enjoyed carrots, peppers, and even spinach. Jono didn't grow potatoes, as they might crawl from the garden and plummet over the cap's edge. Day ebbed to evening atop the great mushroom. The setting sun meant increasing cold.

"I don't suppose you can light fires up here?" Eyna rubbed his shoulders.

22

"No." Jono's sapphire stare was till still strong in the ebbing light. "The shrooms would not like that."

"Ow!" Eyna grabbed his upper arm where Jono had snaked his hand and pinched it. "I get it. No fire. Ever."

"Here is something better."

Jono pulled a sweater woven from the rainbow moss Eyna had seen in the forest. Eyna took it and stared as the fibers acted as prisms in the evening light.

"Yes, it's last vision moss, but it won't digest you." Jono smiled. "The enzymes are long gone. And those aren't the filaments that eat you, anyhow. But it will keep you warm."

"Filaments?" Eyna asked, but the phrase 'eat you' resonated louder in his mind.

"You've never seen it? The refracted rainbow and sweet drops attract prey into its net." Jon explained. "If you can't free yourself from the strong, sticky filaments, the enzymes they release will turn you into goo for it to absorb. Mostly they eat small prey. Birds, flies, clumsy floaks. A bit like a like a spider web of old, but without the spider. The filaments catch light, but they're also better at retaining heat than most furs. Just don't harvest it without shroom spores on hand."

Eyna nodded and put the sweater on. He was almost instantly warm.

"Before its gets too dark—" Jono said and slid over a pouch. He opened it and withdrew a large beetle that began to glow a brilliant yellow-green. "Now, don't let it get away. It will remain docile as long as it's warm." He handed the big, brilliant scarab to the wide eyed Eyna. "They're called kleeks, and they live deep in the clefts between the gills. Sometimes they need to be removed when the spores are due to drift. Too big a colony can encrust part of a gill and cause a rupture. Of course, in my clutch their numbers are quite low."

Eyna smiled at Jono and brought the glowing bug to his lap. He thought he looked like a human camp fire, but the kleek's light didn't flicker.

23

"I assume they glow to daze predators. The upper reaches of the gills are dark. Very dark. They also communicate by sharp clicks. It's some form of enchantment. All kleeks hatched from the same cluster can signal each other instantly. From shroom to shroom and even across leagues."

"How?" Eyna asked.

"I only know that it works, and makes keeping a few worth it. And they taste good."

Eyna wondered if Jono expected him to eat the kleek. He resolved not to disappoint Jono. It couldn't be any worse than what a mud bug ate.

"That bits a joke." Jono chuckled.

Eyna sighed in relief.

"Are these the things that swarm in the gills?"

"No." Jono answered. "Those are bees. That's what I call them, anyway. They appear to have a role in the shrooms' germination. I think they may even be a part of the shrooms, themselves. Like blood cells or other moving tissue within us. Only outside."

Eyna looked at Jono with wide eyes, again.

"Biology. Always interesting. Wouldn't you say?" Jono asked.

"Yeah. I want to be a naturalist." Eyna nodded. "I study nature. Even in libraries."

"Must be some wild libraries. But a laudable pursuit. Have you ever thought of astronomy?"

"Um, no." Eyna said. "You?"

"I think we need more astronomers. Other peoples on other worlds are venturing forth, not on clutches but in ships. Perhaps we will again, one day."

"You think we should abandon the clutches?" Eyna was shocked. He felt his kleek squirm and adjusted his grip on it.

"No. That can never happen. So long as humans draw breath on Sauris, there will be Tenders. But we will need people who understand the stars as humanity did once. Better,

24

perhaps. And perhaps you could be that person to teach us this better knowledge."

"How could I know better knowledge of stars than someone who has traveled among them?" Eyna asked.

"I once learned of mushrooms and tenders without ever having touched a stem." Jono said looking at Eyna. "I'm certain you don't need to touch a star to learn its properties."

Eyna smiled. The sun set on Eyna's trek across and up a small part of his world. For many, his experiences of this day would be an adventure even if not as far flung as Jono's own. The stars of Sauris claimed the sky. Sleep soon claimed Eyna.

Eyna awoke at the base of the giant mushrooms. He stared up at them in shock. Somehow, Jono had brought him down and put him safely outside the world of the clutch. Eyna decided he shouldn't be surprised at anything Jono could do. He was disappointed he would not see dawn from atop the giants. As he moved, he felt a thin sheet of silk over his body begin to tear. Eyna wondered if the spiders helped Jono bring him down, and yet he didn't shudder. Eyna stood. He still wore the moss sweater, and a pouch now hung around his neck. He was at the road that came near the base of the clutch. A woman dressed in the scarlet robes of a Lead Mage sat on the driver's seat of an ox drawn wagon. She smiled at Eyna.

"I'm Iris, young Eyna. Jono has loaned us his wagon. I suggest we both use it to return to Alterwood."

Eyna sighed, but climbed aboard the wagon. Somehow the ride was smooth. The ox hardly slowed when reaching the incline that took the road into the forest. Eyna turned to take a long, last look at the clutch in the distance. It would only be his last look on this day. Eyna would return to Crater Valley. He looked for the smaller mushroom where Jono kept his garden. Reflected light flickered from its summit. Eyna felt his new pouch and withdrew the field glasses Jono used to show him the spiders high on the stem. Eyna brought them to his eyes and kept tapping them until saw Jono flashing sunlight on a signal mirror. Eyna couldn't read the signal, if there was one.

But he could read the knowing smile. Eyna dropped the glasses when he saw Jono turn. Eyna decided that meeting a living legend was a solid consolation to failing to discover a new species. He would keep studying naturalism, and even some astronomy. But he would disappoint Jono on that aspect. Eyna decoded he would never pilot a ship or stare at stars from observatories. He would see them, but through the ethereal envelope of a clutch as it made its transit from Sauris. Eyna would become a Tender. Perhaps he would see Jono again, not only inside his own clutch, but high above the clouds within the Afar.

REVERB

Anne curled a lock of her long, auburn hair in her fingers. She quickly stopped when she spotted an interesting man at the party. Anne had never seen him before. At first he seemed like another party goer who was just a friend of a friend passed in the crowd and never spoken to over loud music. However, as Anne looked at him, he seemed to become more handsome. She decided to speak to the blonde man wearing sunglasses and a leather jacket, even if he looked a bit confused. He wasn't going anywhere. He stood trapped by the gathering crowd against a colorful mural splashed across the cement retaining wall along the driveway. A line of ragged green capped the wall from the sloping lawn above. The outreached grass threatened to jab the man's already tousled hair. Anne thought he could use a comb, and the lawn could use a mow.

"Hi. I'm Anne." She smiled.

The blonde man's head bobbed for a second before looking at Anne. It was as if he was hearing words spoken directly to him for the first time.

"Yeah. Hi." He finally answered.

"You have a name?

"Pete. I think."

"You think?" Anne smiled. She though he really was a bit confused. Maybe he got to the party early and already tapped the backyard keg too hard. Yet, she had been here early and had not seen before now. He seemed in control of his coordination.

"Yeah. I'm sure it's Pete."

"Okay, Pete. What do you do?"

"I'm not sure."

"Really? The beer is that good?" Anne now thought of heading to the backyard, or some other site.

"I don't think I've had it before," the probable Pete answered. "What do you do?"

"I manage a non-profit, patient advocate firm," Anne said. "We coordinate assistance for people who have medical challenges, but don't have anyone at home to help them."

"That sounds right." Pete nodded as if in recollection.

"You work at a non-profit?"

"I think so. Yeah, I'm sure I do."

"Okay." Anne laughed. She looked for an exit, but the crowd had now also trapped her. She looked back at Pete. "So, do you play?"

Anne watched Pete's eyebrows rise over his sunglasses in confusion.

"An instrument." Anne offered. "You could throw a cup in any direction here, and always hit a musician."

"Wow. Um. No. I think." Pete looked over the crowd that was now gathering in the driveway and the yard above. "Do you?"

"Yes. Ellie and I still play. We do a few shows, every so often." Anne smiled as she recalled years of happy memories with her friend and musical collaborator. "Ellie got us a gig next week at the Sun Tractor."

"Ellie?" Pete asked.

"Our beautiful hostess, along with her husband, Don." Anne said. "Do you know them?"

"Don. Right. Don." Pete seemed to suddenly be having memories of his own. The confusion began to ebb from his face. He smiled, and looked back at Anne with more confidence. "So, you run a firm and play music. Nice. I'm impressed. Got any other talents?"

Anne smiled now, not only from amusement.

Ellie laughed. Her friend Davis departed her after dropping his joke, and entered the house in search of Ellie's husband Don and more sets of ears for punchlines. Ellie took a sip from her drink, and noticed Anne talking to a blonde stranger down in the driveway. Body language meant they were not close. Did she need rescuing? And who was this guy?

Curiosity led Ellie down the lawn, through a few greetings, and beside the mural.

"Hey!" Ellie gave Anne a quick pat on the shoulder as if greeting Anne at the party for the first time.

"Hiya, El," Anne gave Ellie a wry smile. "Do you know Pete?"

"Oh, hi, Pete!" Ellie extended a hand.

"You must be Ellie." Pete gently shook her hand.

"Yeah! Nice to meet you." Ellie flashed her electric smile. She knew it would stun most people into a half second of silence and give her the edge in the conversation. "Say, Anne, can I borrow you for minute. About our show. Just a quick sec."

"Sure." Anne said.

They both nodded to Pete who gave a knowing smile.

"There's a keg in the back, bytheway." Ellie chirped with a glance back to Pete.

Anne followed Ellie a few steps away. The crowd noise covered their clandestine chat. For a moment Ellie worried about neighbor noise complaints, but focused on her own curiosity.

"So." Ellie said.

"So, yeah." Anne answered.

"Looking good or just good looking?" Ellie asked.

"Maybe both."

"Looks like he could use a few style tips." Ellie glanced sideways at Pete over her drink.

"Don't they all." Anne said, and wished she had a drink of her own. "I'll bet he'd look really good in a blazer, instead of that leather."

"Yeah. It seems hot, I mean in the temperature sense." Ellie took another sideward sip.

"It would show off his shoulders, better." Anne glanced over at Pete, herself. "Otherwise, he seems nice."

"Not an airhead like Duke. Or was it 'The' Duke." Ellie asked with a devilish version of her smile.

"I'll never live that one down." Anne squinted at Ellie.

"Well, his name was Duke. So you kinda' had to date him." Ellie brought her glass to her sharp smile and sipped.

They both glanced over at Pete. A thousand ideas about him rolled through Anne and Ellie's mind. Missing aspects were added, deleted, and reimagined. His exterior style has stripped and restored, and then remade again. He enjoyed many different careers and fates in the active minds of his observers. It all occurred in the second before Anne thought to mention his previous vacuity.

"There was—"

"Hey, guys!" Lorna made her typical brash entrance with mobile phone extended and camera on. Her penchant had led to capturing some images that the participants did not want recorded on any media, especially the social variety.

"Hey, single girl!" Lorna said to Anne while sweeping her phone towards where Pete had stood. "I saw you talking to Mr. Blonde over—okay, weird."

"What?" Anne and Ellie asked.

"He was just there." Lorna pointed at the mural. "Now he's gone."

"Did he leave?" Anne looked towards the street.

"I didn't see him walk by." Ellie said and glanced around. "No one could leave without us seeing it."

"Nobody gets by me if I'm around." Lorna said.

Anne and Ellie sighed in unison.

Lorna replayed her video with Anne and Ellie watching. Compressed party noise served as the soundtrack of Lorna's bounding documentary of crowd navigation.

"Look, there's blondie." Lorna said pointing at the small screen. "That blazer really shows off his shoulders."

The swerving camera angles showed Pete now wearing a tailored blazer and sporting neatly combed hair. The video then flashed over to Anne and Ellie. As Anne watched the replay, her eyes widened.

"What?" Lorna asked looking at Anne's shock.

"I don't know." Anne breathed. She stared over where Pete had stood.

"Hey, Pete!" Lorna called out. She sprinted to a man with long, brunette hair and no jacket who had been socializing in the driveway for some time.

"Yeah, okay, weird!" Ellie said her stance was frozen as she stood and stared with Anne at the mural.

"Did you hear the audio?" Anne asked.

"Not really. Why?"

"I—"

"You said he should wear a blazer!" Ellie shouted as she recalled Pete's instantaneous wardrobe change on the video.

"Yeah, and I mentioned Aeschylus." Anne shook her head slightly as she also considered Pete's instant transformation.

"Who-sku-lus?"

"The Greek tragedy writer. He asked if I had other talents. I told him I once thought of a career as a writer before music took over. We talked about influences. Aeschylus came up."

"Oh, right. So?"

"So, he didn't know who Aeschylus was. He didn't seem to know much of anything. At first, anyway." Anne took a deep breath. "And then there he is in the video wearing a blazer and talking about Aeschylus."

"OK. Weird." Ellie took a long pull from her drink.

"Yeah. It was like he changed to match thoughts about him. As if we were defining him, somehow."

"Geez!" Ellie nearly leapt from where she stood. "Maybe we did. Maybe he was some sort of, I don't know, some sort of half-created person. Like ghost, but not dead."

"A zombie?" Anne said playfully.

"No!" Ellie gestured passionately with her free hand as she spoke. "Like a shade, a reflection from some alternate world. But just like a reflection, he didn't have all the dimensions. He was part of a world still developing and slipped into ours."

"A guy from a parallel world who likes parties." Anne cocked her left eyebrow at Ellie.

"Who doesn't? But his party was not quite whole, like a low definition video of one."

"Or a note sung far away." Anne relaxed her face and considered Ellie's ideas.

"Okay. I like it!" Ellie chirped.

"So, he needed an amp." Anne added.

"Geez!" Ellie nearly leapt again.

"What?"

"My dad!" Ellie's gaze looked far over the driveway crowd as memories rolled out in her mind. "When he would practice on his drum kit in the basement, he said sometimes hazy images of people appeared. Mom always thought he was just seeing reflections through the garage. Uncle Bert said it was ghosts. But what if it was echoes of people in a parallel universe? The vibration from Dad's drumming somehow made them visible."

"I like the ghost idea, better." Anne said.

"You always had a thing for Bert." Ellie said with a raise of her own eyebrows.

"Oh, c'mon!"

"So Dad said sometimes he would see people sort of appear and disappear at shows." Ellie continued. "We've seen that!"

"Yeah, but a lot of people pop in and out of a show." Anne shrugged. "Some just for a smoke. And I've never seen smoke wear a leather jacket. Or a blazer."

"What about Duke?" Ellie smiled behind her glass.

Anne gave Ellie a narrowed stare.

"Okay. Sorry." Ellie said. "But I'll bet on some Earth there is a party like this one, but just slightly altered."

"And some of the alterations lose information." Anne looked out across the crowd.

"Yeah." Ellie nodded eagerly. "But if they intersect with more fully defined worlds, information gets added."

"So this Pete from an alternate Earth needed us to add details." Anne said enjoying Ellie's zeal. "Like a dress-up doll from the ether."

"Some physicists say parallel worlds happen every moment."

"And they play with dress-up dolls?" Anne asked with a smirk.

"I think so." Ellie flashed her own electric grin.

Anne smiled, too. Before they had met, each was already a fan of fantasy, science fiction, cutting edge scientific theory, and father out concepts. It was not odd for any of those topics to shape their conversations. It was odd that theories of alternate Earths and visitors from them seemed nearly reasonable to explain a man who changed and then vanished with no trace. Perhaps it was not odd at all.

"So, if he came from an alternate world, where did he go?" Anne asked. "Back home?"

"Maybe. If he was a reflection of another Pete, or whoever, maybe he popped into to a more definite Earth once he gained enough information here."

"I suppose an image, or a reflection, can't stay flat if it goes from two dimensions to three." Anne caressed the thick paint of the mural on the cement wall. "It would pop into another plane. I could go for something stronger than pop right now."

"On some Earth right now, we are both enjoying a finely mixed beverage." Ellie said and raised her empty glass.

"Let's go make that one a reality."

Don caught sight of his friend beside the plain cement retaining wall by the driveway. He hustled down his manicured lawn to greet him with another friend in tow.

"Hey, Paul!" Don shouted over the heavy bass line thundering from the band rocking out in the basement. "You seemed to disappear. People thought you left."

"Still here!" Paul smiled.

"I want you to meet someone." Don smiled and stepped aside to reveal a young woman with long, auburn hair.

"Hi. I'm Amy." she said as they shook hands.

Paul and Amy shared a quick smile of shared awkwardness at the blunt introduction that widened into one of mutual charm.

"I like your blazer." Amy said. She thought the sport jacket made him look slim, and hung nicely over his shoulders below a well-combed mass of blonde hair.

Paul had a sudden but unexplained urge to mention Aeschylus.

A short time later, and moved slightly sideways, Ellie and Anne began to play their set at the Sun Tractor tavern. Their characteristic sound of heavy bass and soaring vocals pleased the crowd. Sound waves rolled from voices, instruments, and through amplifiers. The waves continued to roll and echo across the many people, and many places unseen. The image of a young woman in the crowd was reflected across the club's glass doors reverberating from the music. Outside, the woman's reflection pulsated, but without glass. A man passing the parking lot thought he saw a ghostly image for just a moment, and continued walking. In another parking lot outside another club that was nearly identical to where Anne and Ellie played, the image of the young woman took solid form. She was slightly confused as to where she was, and even who she was on this echo of Earth. However, she did know for certain that she liked music with a heavy bass and soaring vocals. She walked forward, following a pulse that expanded her own and other dimensions.

DEMONS, MAIDENS, AND A KITCHEN SINK

The ride was near torture. The hulking machine smashed through small hills rising across the Abduran countryside on linked tracks. Its thunderous passage cut deep ruts across the verdant fields. Inside its creaking armor plates, the human occupants endured swaying, bouncing, and sudden jolts straining their harness straps. King Stephen of Abdura endured the raucous demonstration. Abdura's national lottery had bestowed his monarchy. Before then, he was enjoying work as a plumber. It had taken his twenties and early thirties to settle on a profession he liked and find happiness. And then he was made king. Unless he was found incompetent by a quorum of his advisors, or killed, his sentence as monarch would be indefinite. The jarring ride felt it would last forever.

Stephen never considered smell when thinking of weapons. But aside from the threat to his bones, this one assaulted his nose. It stank like the earthen crawlspace beneath a house with leaking pipes, and a rodent problem. Large rodents. The wall separating the engine housing was solid steel. Yet, it was lousy sound proofing. The engine roared on. Some fumes seeped into the crew's compartment. Worst of all it gave off heat on a hot summer day in a cramped, jolting metal box. Stephen's ceremonial mantelet had become a clinging sheet of wet velvet. He watched the sweaty Major Ashland wrestle with glee at the controls. Ashland's powerful arms wiggled like marionette strings knotted to the levers. Still, he was enjoying himself. His king just wanted it to end. There was a sudden jolt. The juggernaut stopped.

"Gunner!" Ashland turned and bellowed into the turret.

Stephen jumped.

"You may want to cover your ears, your highness!" Ashland barked respectfully at the king, then immediately yelled: "Fire!"

A fraction of a second before Stephen's hands covered his ears, the cannon blasted overhead. The world shook.

Stephen looked to see if the machine named a "juggernaut" had exploded, itself, but it was intact. Better yet, nothing had fallen from his own body. Ashland began shouting with excitement and pointed out the driver's hatch at the elaborate wooden fortification on the facing hilltop. As Stephen nervously swept his tongue through his mouth to find broken or missing teeth, the wooden fort exploded into shards and flames.

"Direct hit!" Ashland spouted. "If that had been an enemy strong hold, they would all be dead, and we could continue into their territory—to victory!" The major smiled broadly. All his teeth were much bigger than the Stephen's own.

"Yes," Stephen said, relived his teeth were still intact. He hoped his hearing would fully return, or at least the ringing in his ears would stop sometime before his retirement years. "Yes, I see the merits of this weapon. The Calvary's research and development arm is, well, impressive. I'm certain this machine can level most anything, not just wooden targets. Now let me out, please. Now."

The main hatch fell open with a resonating clank! Stephen scrambled out, followed by Major Ashland.

"I hope I have convinced you, your highness, that building these juggernauts should be your budgetary priority. The Infantry has given me their full support. I assure your highness, that they will save many soldiers lives."

Stephen thought of the annihilated target. "Our troops. Yes. I have one other project to inspect. But I can't imagine it will be more, well, more destructive than this one."

Again the Major's teeth gleamed front and center before the king. Stephen tried to emulate the Major's enthusiasm, but slipped back into pained acceptance of his reality. Abdura was at war with the only other nation on the planet, Pangea. They had declared war before the national lottery made Stephen king. The hostilities started over fishing rights, but the fighting was mostly on the borderlands. Fishing boats made for a very slow and preoccupied navy. Stephen had been glad he was too old to be a conscript. His daughter still needed a father. Now as king, he was ostensibly in charge of all military operations. Stranger still, his ex wife was Pangea's elected Queen. The war was her reign's defining act. She had left her family and country to find a better career, and evidently more fish.

A shadow fell over the area. A strong wind buffeted the sweaty men. A gigantic, luminous teal bird descended to the countryside several meters away. It's massive body defied gravity through Necrolytic manipulations. The Daedaladon alit on the grass as graceful as a sparrow. Its rider waved from the harness rig, and relaxed the reigns as the bird folded its enormous wings. Stephen's official transportation had arrived. Major Ashland took a moment to admire the radiant, magical bird he had only seen in photographs.

If being king had any real joy, Stephen often thought, it was soaring on the back of the Daedaladon. After his joy ride had ended, Stephen again befell the wrath of his protocol advisor. He protested loudly in the royal water closet.

"The king, in any official function, is to wear the mantelet!"

"In that case, they should have made more than one."

Stephen looked at the sweat-sodden, purple cape held at arm's length by the officious, little man. Not even the rush of air while flying to the palace had dried it out. He would not drape the wet robe over his fresh clothes. It was bad enough someone was in the bathroom whenever he used it. There were some protocols that should remain private. Stephen retrieved a purple towel, clipped on the national amulet, and returned to his avian limousine. He hated to disappoint people. He hated being wet even more. It had been a drawback when he was a plumber.

Earlier, Stephen had soared beneath the sun. Then he descended inside a dank elevator. When he stepped out, sunlight shone only as a dot high overhead. The missile silo was dark place with weak lamplight reflecting off every surface of this new, metal domain. Metal was a pervading theme when dealing with Abdura's military. General Bloomengardt greeted Stephen. Bloomengardt seemed cast from bronze, himself. He commanded Strategic Forces, and served as a key advisor that judged Stephen's competence. Bloomengardt's medals gleamed like the skin of the missile that rose beside them and blocked the sunbeams. The missile halted its ascent. There was a hiss of steam. The echo of great cogwheels locking in place resounded through the silo and Stephen's head. The missile was ready to launch.

"Warheads." General Bloomengardt barked over the echo. "We have the missiles to reach across to Pangea, and the improved radian reflection to target her cities. Now we need the proper warheads to destroy them."

"Weren't the missiles designed with a warhead in mind?"

"Yes, your highness. But the mark IV possesses far less power than the warheads I'd like you to sanction."

"And what warheads are those?"

"Please, your highness, let's confer inside the command suite."

Stephen thought 'suite' was an odd name for a room deep inside a missile silo. The walls of hewn rock did not change his mind. Stephen smiled at two of the greatest minds on the planet, and Abdura's Principle Academicians. He nervously adjusted the national amulet he wore, and remembered it was pinned to a towel. Stephen knew Professor Solerno. He had briefed him on all pertinent technical issues. Stephen had taken pride in remaining awake throughout the lectures. Professor Sonenberg was still more famous than the younger Solerno. Once, Sonenberg wrote all knowledge disseminated to Abdura's populace. If he had actually done so, it might explain his arthritic hands, but not his enormous eyebrows.

The transcription of knowledge dated back to the very first human civilization on the planet called Pangea, if you lived in Pangea. However, Abdurans called the world Portis. That difference in names, if not name calling, was another tradition lost in time. Lost too was a great deal of knowledge from that first civilization. Rediscovery and handled-down specifications created an entire world of patchwork technology, magical constructs, and the indigenous results of their fusion.

It was still a practiced tradition that business took place before social introductions. It was expected that eminent people were known to everyone, and needed to conserve time. Nevertheless, Stephen always attempted an exchange of smiles to show he would be friendly if there ever was time to socialize with the people who breezed through his official life.

"Your highness!" Solerno piped. "You know the Daedaladon well. I'm sure you've heard of the shrieking loons of Lake Tsongas. A bad tourism decision by your predecessor, but another example of the biological application of Necrolytic methods."

"I'm familiar with those creatures, Professor." Stephen said. "I understood we were to talk of new warheads."

"Demons." Sonenberg spat.

"Demons?"

"Yes. Are you also familiar with their onslaught twenty years ago?" Bloomengardt asked.

"Yes." Stephen nodded while recalling the national nightmare. "They are an even worse example of Necrolytic life. But they were all destroyed, and banned from creation. Right?"

There was a moment of silence as Stephen raised his own eyebrows. Sonenberg did likewise, hiding his forehead almost completely.

"The fine print of that decree states that civilians may not store, employ, or create demons. The military, however, is exempt from that decree."

"Oh--kay." Stephen stretched out the two syllables and tried to fathom where this discussion was heading. His scalp muscles tightened. He felt his ears pull back. They still rang.

Bloomengardt stood beside the two academics. "In short, your highness, we want you to sanction the deployment of demons within the warhead compartments of our intercontinental missiles."

"Oh--kay."

"The warheads will burst over the Pangean cities, releasing the demons to attack." Solerno instructed. "The resulting plague of fiends and chaos will equal the destruction of several more missile strikes."

"Strategically," Bloomengardt interjected, "the demon attacks will consume more Pangean time and materiel to combat the onslaught, and in their home cities, not just on the frontline. This plan has great strategic value."

"Oh--kay." Stephen took a deep breath. "But where do we get the demons? Aren't they all dead, and illegal?"

"No," Bloomengardt answered. "And as I explained to your highness before: no. The military captured a host of demons during their original onslaught. We've kept them in suspension. Now, we have a good reason to reanimate them, and use the heinous creatures to the advantage of this great nation."

"Oh--kay."

"Excellent!" Bloomengardt barked. "Then we have your authorization?"

"I'm sure it will be a very destructive plan, General. Each new weapon I've seen today has been a staggering escalation over the last."

"We serve our nation as best we can." Bloomengardt replied.

Solerno nodded his support of the General's sentiment. Sonenberg stared suspiciously at Stephen's boots. He then studied his own footwear.

"Before we launch, I think I will try to contact Pangea's Queen one final time."

"Your highness, I implore you to put aside sentimental ties. Our nation needs swift action."

"I agree, General. But before we annihilate enemy cities, perhaps we should see if they will come back to negotiations."

Silence and averted glances answered Stephen's suggestion.

"General," Stephen sighed, "load the demons onto the missiles."

"Ah, we will need to discuss one, final detail before we launch, your highness." Solerno said with unease.

"You mean, before I grant permission to launch."

"Yes, your highness." Bloomengardt looked satisfied with his victory, so far. "This detail can wait."

Breton, the Advisor of Interior and Foreign Affairs, met Stephen at the palace. His slick, flat hairstyle contrasted sharply with Stephen's wind-whipped mane. Such hair was the accepted style of all monarchs since the Daedaladon's creation. Breton's pained expression reminded Stephen of his own headache. He did not anticipate it easing any time soon.

"The communications parlor is ready, your highness." Breton droned. "The Pangeans have honored the Articles of Hostility, and have not destroyed the transcontinental cable. We have contacted their leadership, as you requested."

"Mythilda will make me wait, no doubt."

"Was it always so?"

Breton's informality surprised Stephen. Perhaps it was a sign of acceptance, even trust, or just fatigue.

"I suppose. Mythilda was always a bit imperious."

"And now she is an enemy queen."

"Yes." Stephen was lost for a moment in reflection of another life. "She must be quite happy. Now."

As they walked to the communications parlor, Stephen looked down at the polished marble floor. The floor of his old home was dented Formica. Mythilda always loathed its rosy color. Stephen remembered how hours of motivational necrograms inspired her desire for success and power. Mythilda could not see her ascent ever occurring within

Abdura's society, so Mythilda emigrated to Pangea. Alone. She left Stephen and their daughter to find their own sense of happiness. Happenstance, or some quirk of magic, placed them at odds. Again. Now the consequence of their actions was far greater in scale.

Stephen's reminiscence ended as he sat in the plush seat before the viewscreen. The seal of Pangea beamed from its glassy surface. He whipped off the towel from his shoulders, and pinned the royal amulet beneath his collar.

"They hold elections to find their leaders in Pangea, Breton. Do you think that would work here?"

Breton's cheeks flexed left to right. "The lottery has worked all right, so far."

Stephen took that as a mild vote of confidence. "Well, thank you Breton."

Breton, lost in thought, only gave a shrug and sideward glance. Stephen did not ask what those thoughts were, and motioned to the technician seated across the room at the control panel.

"We're waiting for them, sire." The technician answered.

"Of course we are." Stephen massaged his forehead. He wondered if he could reach an accord with his ex-wife, the self-proclaimed Warrior Queen. Should he mention their daughter, Merry Ann, who was now a maiden? Perhaps he should have brought her here. But would Mythilda acknowledge him as an equal? He would not want to be embarrassed in front of his daughter. Mythilda's round face flashed onto the screen.

"You look desperate, Stephen. Is that why you've called? Abdura is ready to capitulate?"

"No. I hoped to restart negotiations. Nice to see you, by the way."

"Our negotiations will be on the battlefield. I almost pity you, Stephen. How you became king demonstrates the

42

Abdura's corruption. How can you fail to see that Pangea will be victorious?"

"Mythilda, you're not giving a speech to your subjects. Let's put the rhetoric aside. Surely there is a way to end this war."

"Surrender."

"I can't do that."

"Is your power as king so impotent that you can't make decisions?"

"Mythilda, that's ridiculous. You know I can't just give up. There must—"

"I refuse to be insulted, Stephen! Your diplomacy is as feckless as your warcraft. Spare your subjects humiliation and resign. Surrender, first."

"Mythilda, let's focus on peace. On reason. If we review the issues that started—"

"I am focused on peace. Peace through victory. Only then can my people be safe from Abduran treachery. Peace will be when there is no Abdura!"

Stephen heard cheering voices in the background through the speaker. Mythilda's image vanished. He stared at the blank screen.

"It was a noble effort, your highness."

Stephen looked at Breton and sighed. "Thank you. Please, contact General Bloomengardt." Stephen had small epiphany. "After that, send for Major Ashland, and the Exchequer Principal."

Dinner usually meant an end to national affairs for the day, but not always. Tonight he entertained General Bloomengardt and the two interesting Academicians at the palace. He thought of the massive weapons awaiting blast off as he stared at the candelabra. Stephen didn't understand why the house staff still set the table with candelabras and candlesticks. It seemed an act that kept going from tradition's inertia. Electric lamps provided enough light, but bleached the rich colors of the dining hall tapestries. However, the ornate wax candles were so old now that he would never imagine striking a match anywhere near them. Still, he would soon fire missiles against Pangean cities. He sighed. An odd thought entered his mind: how many demons can dance on the tip of a warhead?

"Now, General, Professors, before dessert, what was that final detail before the launch?"

"In short, your highness," Bloomengardt answered, "we want to clone maidens."

"Clone young, pure girls?" Stephen's forehead furrowed. "My daughter is a maiden! What possible military application would that serve?"

He dreaded the answer.

"Demons!" Sonenberg spat.

"Demons?"

"Yes." Bloomengardt continued. "The only way demons are stopped, is to sacrifice maidens to them. Once they're tranquil, enough firepower can be brought to point-blank range to them to kill them."

"I see." Stephen said, but still tried to grasp Bloomengardt's ultimate point. "But we want them to be destructive—is Pangea planning similar strike on us?"

"No, your highness. They posses no long-range missiles. At the moment."

"Oh--kay. No, wait. What about the maidens of Pangea? Can they stop the demon attack?"

"You are more perceptive than the last one." Sonenberg drew closer across the table to study Stephen's head.

"Sire, we considered such an obstacle." Solerno spoke up. "Even assuming one hundred percent chastity, the demographics of Pangea indicate there aren't enough young women in their population to stop all the demons."

"But--" Stephen sighed on making a realization. "Once they've raided Pangea, the demons will attack us here."

"Precisely, your highness." Bloomengardt nodded. "And we had better be prepared once they do."

44

Stephen massaged his forehead. "So we trade one war for a potential apocalypse. And I've already told you to load the demons onto the missiles."

"And we have complied with your orders. Now we need your leadership to take the next step: Securing the future of Abdura."

"Can you disarm the missiles?"

Bloomengardt paused. Solerno's face wrinkled in disgust at the prospect. Sonenberg now probed his own skull.

"It would be difficult." Bloomengardt finally replied. "The demons are already waking."

"So we'd better launch soon." Stephen sat back in his chair.

"It is strongly advisable, sire." Bloomengardt said. "Very soon."

Solerno and Sonenberg nodded energetic agreement.

Stephen inhaled to voice swift consent. He held his breath. The events he had set in motion swirled in his mind. Making a decision as king had always felt more about pleasing important people in ornate rooms or secret locations. The order to launch demons mounted on missiles against enemy cities felt as easy as clearing a clogged pipe. Now he felt pressure building. Seconds felt as if they were shuddering hours spent inside one of Ashland's juggernauts. He looked at his distinguished, increasingly impatient, but silent guests.

Stephen never wanted to be a soldier, let alone a king. As king, his decisions impacted the lives of all soldiers, and two nations. Soldiers were images of strength and dedication. Maidens were a traditional image of innocence and grace, and now also an important factor in war. Stephen decided he would define the image of king in his own mind, not the judging eyes squinting at him across the table.

"No." Stephen finally exhaled.

A murmur of shock reverberated off the tapestries. "Sire--!" Bloomengardt began.

"No to cloning maidens, General."

"But, sire!" The shout erupted in unison.

"I understand we must launch those missiles." Stephen continued. "You've forced my hand. I suppose I shouldn't be shocked I was outmaneuvered by a General."

Stephen found the resolve to stare at Bloomengardt, who pursed his lips and slowly lowered his fork.

"Your highness--"

"Do not do it again, General. I need to trust you. Or your replacement."

"Understood, sire."

"But you will not clone maidens."

"Then you doom both countries!" Sonenberg spat without a hint of formal address.

"Again, no." Stephen pointed at both Sonenberg and Solerno. "You will have time before the devastation we're sending to Pangea comes back at us. Use it. There must be some important reason why maidens appease demons. Find it. Mass produce that. Not living people."

"Well, yes, there is something other than flesh that acts as appeasement," Sonenberg said while vibrating in his plush chair. "But this, this maiden essence--!"

"We don't know what it is!" Solerno finished. "Let alone synthesizing it en masse! If the research takes too long--!"

"Find it." Stephen cut in. "If your briefings on simulacratic theory were accurate, on both biological and magical aspects, then mass cloning itself would likely take too long. Even so, I'm not sending hundreds, thousands, or perhaps more young women to be sacrificed, even if they're born of some Necrolytic concoction. So long as they draw breath and think, they're citizens of this nation, and I am sworn to protect them. I'm not going to fail that duty, even if my throne came by lottery. I'm sure you won't fail in yours."

Stephen stared at the wide-eyed Gen. Bloomengardt and the shocked academics.

"When dealing with a clog, a plumber doesn't replace all the pipes." Stephen said. "You fix the one pipe. The one problem. It's not in the foundation, not the roof. You focus on the location of the clog."

Stephen was happy to see dessert served at last. His guests were now lost to their own thoughts. He didn't know if they understood his clog analogy or not. He didn't care. What they had offered as a solution had become a bigger problem. Stephen hoped his decision would stop the escalation, at least for this issue. He thought of his daughter, Merry Ann. Perhaps she at least would be proud of him. Stephen eagerly thrust a fork into a slice of rhodulaberry torte.

Stephen stood for the war briefing. He felt he thought better while standing. He also felt more comfortable in ridiculous, ceremonial clothes and making world altering decisions. Still, he pared the meetings down to only essential personnel. It kept the judgmental eyes to a minimum. The conference room of Strategic Command was surprisingly small. The command itself was still new and growing, and smelled of drying paint. Stephen could foresee long-range war as the future of all conflict. Yet, if it was true Abdura was close to victory, would there be a need for war at all? He silently hoped this meeting would answer that question.

Solerno and Bloomengardt nodded to their king. Stephen was surprised to see Sonenberg, who stood next to a set of colorful graphs. A pointer was poised rapier-like in his left hand.

"Your highness," Bloomengardt began, "I'm proud to report that all our missiles struck deep into Pangea's industrial and population centers. However, I must also report that the guidance systems were not as accurate as hoped. Nevertheless, the demon payloads have inflicted great havoc upon our enemy."

"I see," Stephen studied the charts carefully. His brow furrowed. Although Sonenberg was poised to explain, Stephen's alarm did not come from confusion.

"This chart shows a decrease in demon destruction at eight hours after launch." Stephen said, and looked at the next set of graphs. "According to this one, two hours ago their activity stops. What happened?"

Sonenberg tossed his pointer aside. His hopes for lengthy dissertation had vanished with Stephen's comprehension of his charts.

Bloomengardt stepped in. "Your highness, I regret to inform you that the enemy has apparently used a heretofore unknown stockpile of maidens to appease the demons."

"Stockpile?" Stephen's voice rose to a most unroyal shriek. "Of Maidens?"

"Yes, sire."

"How do you stockpile young women?" How do you stockpile demons? Stephen thought to himself.

"Unknown, sire. However, our spies witnessed maidens brought in by the truck load. Evidently they were some form of simulacrum, or clone."

Bloomengardt smiled to himself as if being proven right. His next point made his face fall into a near sulk.

"The Pangeans also used some form of aerosol. Spies described it as smelling similar to hair spray, or florid shampoo. This also appeased the demons, just after they incinerated or ate the spray teams." Bloomengardt smiled again.

"An essence of maiden, it seems." Stephen beamed.

"Yes. And, your highness—" Bloomengardt halted for a second when glancing at Stephen's wide smile. "Avian reconnaissance has confirmed massive truck traffic in the assaulted locations."

"So," Stephen paused. He stopped gloating, and suddenly wanted a chair. "This attack wasn't the war ender we hoped for."

"No. But there is more news, your highness."

"Of course." Stephen braced himself and stiffened his lips. "And it's bad."

"Potentially. Our intelligence indicates the Pangeans are not destroying the demons."

Bloomengardt let that statement sink in. The demons were still alive, appeased and in Pangean control.

"I see." Stephen's eyes drifted over the charts' vibrant colors. "They have no missiles, but a lot of trucks, apparently. Assuming the Pangeans can make the demons mad again, once they've moved them, how soon can they get them to the frontline?"

"Factoring in their current disorder, and our own tactical bombing at the front, the Professors and I estimate two weeks."

"How are close are you on determining the link between demons and maidens?" Stephen asked. "I'd like to know at least what the Pangeans discovered before those monsters are gnawing on the palace doors."

"We've establish a research group, King Stephen." Solerno answered. "We will find the answer, as you directed."

"A better answer." Sonenberg added.

"Excellent." Stephen sighed with slight relief. "General, I want you to work with Major Ashland. We will need his machines at the front, quickly. Coordinate whatever support is necessary to get those weapons massed."

"We can coordinate artillery and aircraft in support of his juggernauts, your highness. Strategic and Calvary commands have been working out the details since you approved and expanded his program."

"That, General, is good news."

Stephen didn't mind the long nights his royal duties required. Usually they occurred in a surprisingly small office. There, two of Breton's officers assisted him. They were called royal aides. However, their presence essentially trapped him in the small office and made them feel like prison guards. The sweeping masses and towers of documents defied the room's ability to contain them. Stephen wondered if a spell worked to keep the walls from bursting. The expanse of paperwork hid what he assumed was an ornate and very sturdy desk beneath it. Atop all of that was a chaotic dance of colliding necrogram images of department officials requesting, among other matters, more paperwork. Stephen felt some joy of liberation when the occasionally clashing pair of Solerno and Sonenberg requested his presence for a secret meeting.

Stephen left the palace with his security force under the cloak of night. Agents wore disguises en route. Stephen was glad to see an agent dressed as a plumber. Although the man's clean fingernails and stain-free work clothes looked slightly inauthentic. Stephen glanced at his own finger nails. For a moment he was surprised to see them completely clean. His agents swept him into Abdura's Fourth Great National Laboratory. The first three had exploded, or fell into sudden, unexplained pits. Inside, the Laboratory's Biological College was a vast network of white halls, multi-story classrooms, and sealed, sterile labs. Within one of those labs, Stephen found himself before a makeshift curtain of white sheets. Behind them came the occasional sound of liquid slapping against glass. It was unsettling. And so were the two men standing before the white sheets.

"Welcome, your highness." Solerno said with a genuine smile.

Sonenberg launched straight into his speech with a hop. "To understand the link between maidens and demons, we needed to fully understand demons. From the first molecule, on up."

"Um, but you would need a demon to do that." Stephen said while nervously peering at the white sheets.

"Exactly!" They replied in a duet.

"Oh--kay."

"We'd launched all the stored ones on rockets, sire." Sonenberg said.

"Missiles." Solerno corrected.

Sonenberg opened his mouth as if to yell and aimed a finger as a spearhead at Solerno. Stephen halted the assault.

50

"Yes, I know. Go on."

"So, we took demon samples—" Solerno began.

"And made a demon!" Sonenberg shouted.

A bolt of fear shot through Stephen's mind. Another wave slapped at glass behind the sheets. He wondered if he should have brought his security detail. Should he just bolt and run?

"Well, that was the goal." Solerno said calmly, but while looking at the floor. "But, instead—"

"Recall, sire, you said we could not clone maidens. Demons were not prohibited!" Sonenberg thrust his face close to Stephen's head. His expression both beseeched and admonished as folds of skin flexed over his older bones.

"So, you cloned a demon." Stephen leaned backwards. His alarm focused momentarily on Sonenberg, but then back at the sheets. "But is it alive! Here?"

"It's here. It's not alive." Solerno answered.

"And it's not a demon." Sonenberg added. "Not really. Well, mostly not."

"Then what is it? Wait!" Stephen suddenly noticed a keen resemblance between Solerno and Sonenberg. "Professors, have you actually ever cloned anything—or anyone?"

Solerno and Sonenberg looked at their king sheepishly. The elder Sonenberg turned smiling at Solerno, who uncomfortably returned his gaze. Despite the age difference, Stephen's now grasped there was likely little else different between then, from the first molecule on up. Sonenberg tweaked Solerno's cheek. He recoiled indignantly.

Stephen drew a deep breath. "Okay. You have. Successfully. So, what is the reason I'm here?"

Sonenberg's enormous eyebrows pitched high.

"It turns out, there is a link. A very important link." Solerno furthered. "The cloning attempts have been, well, technically speaking—"

"Bizarre." Sonenberg finished.

"Oh. Really?" Stephen sighed. He felt his forehead tighten.

"Yes, really, your highness." Sonenberg nodded. His eyebrows bobbed a second more slowly than his head.

"In attempting to accelerate the clones' maturation, we accidentally, well nearly, but not quite—" Solerno halted.

"We believe in safety, you know." Sonenberg interjected.

Stephen thought of the destructive fates of the previous three Great Laboratories, and became more nervous.

"We almost created maidens." Solerno finished.

"Maidens?" Stephen's shock fluttered his voice near to laughter.

"Yes, King Stephen." Sonenberg said. "While growing large, horrific, demons, we instead nearly created young, pure women. Some almost attractive. Quite lithe in fact. And the breasts—"

A shoulder slap from Solerno ended the elder professors lurid musing.

Stephen's squinted. He was looking at the eminent minds of his country. If not for the lottery that made him king, he would never have the privilege of meeting such esteemed people. Yet, he looked at them now with deepening disbelief. Stephen longed for the time when this would simply be a matter to read in the news texts, then dismiss or ponder, knowing the decision was made long before the printers set their typefaces. Today he had no such luxury. Any actions to come from this were his alone. And these odd fellows were the people that would guide him, a former plumber, now monarch. His brow drew tighter.

"Are you sure?" Stephen asked, but had little doubt the proof would come at the expense of his hopes.

Solerno tugged away the white sheets. They fell to reveal three large glass cylinders holding grotesque, near human shapes. The first contained a hulking menace. Long wisps of hair floated about the head of the monstrosity. It was the lone human trait. Armored plates erupted from its alligator-like skin. The face was a hideous gargoyle's snarl. The second cylinder held a swollen but recognizably female form. However, knurled spines emerged from its vertebrae and at each, massive joint. The third held the body of a young, almost fully human woman, but with solid emerald eyes and protruding, jagged teeth. The same solid green eyes glimmered in all three. Stephen was glad they were motionless, perhaps dead. Or were they?

"They never became fully animate." Solerno said as if to quell Stephen's visible nausea. "Of course, we used Necrolytic methods. I doubt purely biological attempt would produce any results. I've begun working on accelerating growth by influencing only time without altering physical or genetic structures."

"So, what I thought was a hellish monster is actually just a perverted human?"

"I'm certain demons were originally created by accident, while trying to duplicate the most beautiful kind of human." Sonenberg added. "Some researchers might find the deviation more valuable. The aberration becomes the focus."

"The fact that demons can become maidens is, perhaps, similar to humans eventually evolving from fish." Solerno said.

"Yes. And they respire in liquid. Now we breathe gas!" Sonenberg spat with an exaggerated shrug and widened eyes as if something had gone wrong in the transition.

"Fish." Stephen exhaled. He thought of the swimming hulks and whorls of spines he liked to gawk at in the royal aquariums. Larger versions swam in the open oceans. They now seemed one of the least strange things he'd seen while king.

Solerno gently tugged the back of Sonenberg's coat, who had taken to peering attentively up Stephen's nostrils. Stephen instinctively scratched his nose.

"Here we added punctuation to the altered evolution." Solerno said. "Necrolysis—Magic—is a method to imbue information from one system to another. It manipulates other information systems, like DNA. After all, everything is ultimately information. Magic allows its transfer without the constraints of the physical world."

"Constraints." Stephen sighed. "Sometimes they are like clogs. Sometimes, they are like valves."

"Sire?" Solerno asked.

"Sometimes you need to have a flow." Stephen said. "Other times, a shut off."

"There is flow of information we now understand, sire."

Stephen looked at Solerno and now wondered if that were truly possible.

"Now that we've reversed the process of how demons were created, we've theorized why maidens appease them. They are, in a sense, the opposing sides of the same quasi-physical spectrum. They are epi-existentially linked."

"Of course, this does little to help living maidens, or any Abdurans, currently." Sonenberg added.

The images of both young women and hideous, chitinous beasts exchanged places in Stephen's mind. Odd arcs of logic careened in Stephen's head, and eventually fell into a single helix.

"Professors!" Stephen shouted, causing both men to jump. "If demons are altered maidens, can you alter the demons back into maidens?"

There was a long pause from the academics. Then, "I don't know," left their mouths in unison.

"Find out, gentlemen. Quickly."

"We will, sire." Sonenberg assured, and nodded. Again his eyebrows followed in delayed motion to his head.

"To that end—" Solerno's question ebbed as Stephen's questioning stare focused on him. Solerno leaned back. His head hit a glass cylinder. He instantly jumped back and glanced at the monster within it. He looked back at Stephen and finished his query. "For the sake of furthering this research, may we have your allowance to clone at least one maiden?"

Stephen squinted. His expression nearly flexed into an angry stare.

"Just one?" Sonenberg pleaded.

Stephen closed his eyes. He massaged his forehead, and said "I have a headache."

"I can fix that." Sonenberg reached into his coat pocket and began fumbling deep inside it.

Stephen waved him off. "No. I'll keep it, for now. At least I can understand where it came from." He looked at the aberrations within the glass cylinders and sighed.

"If it can save lives, then I suppose I should allow it. We need to stop the demons for both countries, and perhaps for all time. All right. Clone a maiden. Just one. And please! Don't confuse the original maidens with their copies!"

"There really won't be any real difference." Sonenberg shrugged. "Theoretically--"

"We won't, King Stephen!" Solerno interjected. "We are as good at paperwork as we are at combining science and magic."

Stephen worried that was true. The result of his approval could come back and bite him, perhaps literally. He quickly mused on bureaucracy, sorcery, and cloning. The word 'triplicate' suddenly had several new meanings for him.

"And--!" Stephen found himself waving a finger. He looked to see that it was only his index finger, and continued. "Don't mount her on a warhead, or feed anyone to anything. Be humane—human! Please!"

"As you wish, sire." Solerno nodded and smiled. His own eyebrows stayed in sync with his head.

"A fish," Stephen uttered as he slowly turned from the scientists.

"Sire?" Solerno asked.

"Out of water." Stephen furthered, and left the lab.

In the throne room, Ashland's teeth were the same size, but circumstance reduced his smile. The brass on his uniform had grown by order of his king, whom he addressed.

"Our 'nauts have kept the enemy at bay, sire. Our new guns are capable of destroying them at close range. But we cannot train our soldiers in armored warfare fast enough, nor build enough 'nauts and guns to counterattack, even with the increased funding your highness has provided. The industrial plants just don't have enough workers to expand production further. You have my deepest apologies, sire."

"I understand, Colonel Ashland. Certainly we would be in deeper trouble were it not for your machines and bravery." Stephen said, rising from the throne. It was an uncomfortable chair.

"Thank you, sire. At times, we are able to confuse the demons into assaulting the Pangean forces following them. Now their troops keep a greater distance from the demons, and that makes stopping them slightly easier. All the enemy breakthroughs have been stopped."

"Hold the line as best you can, Colonel. I'll see if I can buy you some time."

"What other options do we have, sire?"

"Perhaps sending conscripts to the industrial sector, in addition to the infantry. Otherwise, I'm not certain. But I'm willing to try almost anything, Colonel."

"By your leave, your highness, I will now return to the front."

"There is a place for you at my dinner table, Colonel. But you may go if you feel it's best."

"I shall eat with my troops, sire. But thank you."

Ashland bowed and departed. The idea that he could make it back to the front in time for dinner made it feel uncomfortably close for Stephen. Tonight he would see his daughter. That brightened his mood as he walked to the dining hall.

Merry Ann and Breton waited for the king to take his seat. Once he did the servants poised against the tapestries dished the up steaming plates of vegetarian entrées. Stephen would have preferred well-grilled beef. He could eat the real thing as king. However, tonight he wished his daughter to feel at home.

"Do you think, father, that Pangea will ever be open to peace negotiations again?"

Stephen smiled at his daughter's question. It seemed to hold the same earnest hope he once held. He looked at Merry Ann for a time before he answered. She didn't look much like her mother. Of that he was glad. And that the children of Abduran rulers held no title themselves. Nevertheless, her free college education was a nice perk of his office.

"I've tried, Merry Ann. We keep the communications cable intact. But their leader is quite obdurate."

"Would it continue to be so if you sent a living delegation? Not one of necrograms, or through electronic means, but living negotiators to meet and talk face to face."

"Even if I thought that would work," especially after the demon attacks, Stephen thought, "who would volunteer?"

"I would," Merry Ann chimed.

"No." Stephen replied immediately.

"I've studied communications, father. And I wouldn't be alone."

"Dear Merry Ann," Stephen inhaled deeply. "I don't care if you took a company of Royal Commandos. No."

"I think you should consider who would accompany me, father. It might change your mind, and the minds of Pangea's leaders."

"Pangeans care nothing of negotiations. Their leader—" Stephen nearly spat out the queen's name, but he chose to keep Mythilda unnamed and abstract. Merry Ann knew who the Pangean queen was, but Stephen didn't wish her confusing the adamant enemy leader with the same person who once begrudgingly baked her holiday cakes. "They do not wish peace talks, Merry Ann. Pangea has made that quite clear in direct contact with me."

"I simply ask you to meet with the other members of the delegation I propose, father."

Stephen's brow tightened. He did not like this dish at all.

"This delegation might at least cause a change in Pangean tactics to more conventional means in the battlefield, sire." Breton surprised his king. "And that would favor us."

"You Breton? You've seen my efforts first hand!"

"Don't blame him, father. I showed him the delegation earlier. Please, just meet with us all."

Stephen dropped his fork, and rested his face in his left hand. "I assume they are outside this room." He looked at Breton who nodded sheepish affirmation. "Send them in. Set a place for each of them. Why not?"

Merry Ann left the hall and returned with her delegation. Stephen bolted upright. Suddenly his past orders had an intensely personal impact. Each clone of Merry Ann smiled back at Stephen, as if to ease his astonishment. All four maidens were dressed in the same blue flower-pattern dress. Three appeared slightly younger than one. However, their appearance was so closely identical that he could not be certain who was the original Merry Ann.

"As you can see, they may rethink their commitment to using demons." Breton smiled.

"Why wouldn't they keep doing so, even if we've created a new method to placate the monsters?" Stephen replied. "And I certainly will not send you to do that! Any of you!"

"Nor do any of us wish to die, father." The third Merry Ann from Stephen's left said. "We think we have a unique ability to reach Queen Mythilda, our mother. Our very existence had a number of ramifications, both personal and war related."

"You're telling me?" Stephen squeaked. "Which one of you is my daughter?"

"All of us," was the united reply.

Stephen leaned against the table. The shock had ebbed. He understood why Merry Ann volunteered for cloning. What else could she do as the king's only child? Now he prepared to battle with his quadrupled daughter, and it was obvious Breton liked their dangerous plan.

"Breton, would you please excuse us. Everyone but my daughter please leave."

"As you wish, sire." There was noticeable disappointment in Breton's voice as he rose to follow the staff out. All four Merry Anns remained.

Stephen waited for the door to fully close. "If you will not tell me which one of you is my daughter, how can I send any of you?"

"Does it matter, father?"

"Yes."

"We are all the same, father."

"No. Only one of you has studied communications. I doubt accelerated aging also imparted my daughter's knowledge."

"Actually, Professor Sonenberg was done well imparting wisdom onto us through Necrolytic techniques."

"Ah ha! Then you are a clone!" Stephen pointed to the forth maiden. "Merry Ann would not need any knowledge imparted of things she already knows."

The other three Merry Ann's gave looks of disappointment at the forth.

"Still, father," The third said, "we are all committed to this cause, and wish to share the burden equally."

"And I wouldn't send a clone of mine to do something I would not do myself." Stephen paused to consider if that made sense. "And I will not send you to do something that may mean your death."

"You send troops into battle, to die." The second countered.

"Actually, we send them to kill the enemy, and sometimes they unfortunately die while doing so. And you, young maiden, are no soldier."

"Why should that matter, father? I still want to serve Abdura. Like you."

"It matters because you are my daughter. My duties as father supersede those of being king."

"That's not fair, father."

"I agree. Nor was your ambush of me."

All Merry Anns became hushed. Stephen smiled as all four young maidens scowled. He remembered all the hard decisions he had made as a father. Now he faced the same frustration quadrupled. He had one strategy yet to play. It would require a tape recorder, and the unwitting aid of his ex-wife.

"I can make no promises, but I'll call your mother. If she will agree to peace talks, only then will I send you."

"Thank you father," the second Merry Ann said. "I don't really remember mother, but maybe we can all appeal to her maternal side."

Or overwhelm it, Stephen thought while looking at all four of his daughters. Then he wondered if the free college benefit also covered clones.

"Are you certain you want to do this, again?" Breton asked Stephen as he entered the communications parlor. His tone of voice was a mixture of concern and repulsion.

"Yes." Stephen said in the same tones.

"They have not shown the courtesy of facing us. Contact has been voice only."

Stephen eased himself into the chair facing the viewscreen, and mused. If Mythilda felt she held the upper hand, perhaps she would be more willing to negotiate. Then again, when did she ever concede the disadvantage? Or, perhaps his technicians could trace the location and find where Mythilda was. A new generation of missiles was waiting to be tested. One of them might reach the coordinates found through the trace. That plan was underhanded and vindictive. No doubt Mythilda would do it herself, if she had the technology. He would try the path of reason. Surely they could both agree this

60

war had gone too far and too long, and they could start an earnest dialogue. Mythilda's face appeared. It drove out Stephen's faint hope, and not because of her scowl.

"You look, well, different, Mythilda." Stephen eyed her new pallid green complexion, and the jagged plates emerging from her cheeks.

"I'm undergoing a change. All my subjects are. We are becoming more like demons to acquit ourselves better in the battlefield. I thank you for granting us this ability."

"You are all becoming demons?"

"No. Only demon-like. It is a temporary measure. My necrologists tell me the effects are fully reversible."

"Well, I was told cloning would be easy, and that radain telemetry was a foolproof targeting system."

"What is cloning telemetry?"

"Um, never mind. Mythilda, why would you tell me about your plans? It undermines the tactical surprise."

"With my subjects becoming living weapons, this war will soon be over. Capitulate."

"Our juggernauts are doing well. But the war has reached an impasse. Perhaps we could end the conflict sooner through a negotiated truce."

"Stephen, Stephen." Mythilda shook her mutated head. "You always came to me when things overwhelmed you. I can only imagine your nation has survived your reign on the backs of its bureaucrats. So once again, I'll help you. Surrender and I'll see that you never have to work again. Spare your subjects humiliation, Stephen. My citizens will eat you if you don't yield. Now."

"I suppose at this point there is no point in telling you why I called."

"I would not be interested unless it was full surrender."

"Do you remember Merry Ann?"

"Of course, Stephen."

"Do you ever regret leaving her behind?"

"She was one of the many sacrifices I made for personal growth. And I did grow. I became queen of this magnificent country. And it will grow, too. And eat yours."

"Wouldn't you spare your daughter? If Pangea is becoming a race of demons, how can she be safe on this world?"

"Sacrifices, Stephen. I told you they are needed for growth. All of Abdura must be sacrificed. I see that more clearly now than before."

"Then she is no different?"

"I grow weary of this useless discussion. If you thought you could sway me with emotional attacks, then you remain a foolish, simple, man. I suppose it is fitting you lead Abdura. You are all the same."

"I see. Well, good luck Mythilda. As we were speaking, we found your location. A missile is on its way. And your mighty nation has no defense against it."

Mythilda's green eyes grew wide. She bolted from her seat. The screen went blank.

"Sire?" the technician approached Stephen nervously. "You didn't instruct us to—"

"Don't worry." Stephen smiled. "I just wanted to win this little battle. And see if their queen could still run."

Stephen enjoyed a roguish chuckle with the technicians. That part he would edit from the tape for the Merry Anns.

"It's three-thirty—in the morning!" Stephen screeched. "I went to bed only an hour ago!"

Stephen looked at Breton standing over the royal bed. His black hair sat pushed into a ramp atop his head. Light from the hallway glinted at its apex. Obviously he also had been asleep not long ago. The four Royal Sentries stood at his sides. The contrast of Breton's rumpled pajamas and the Sentries polished uniforms entertained Stephen's groggy mind.

"My apologies for disturbing you, sire." General Bloomengardt entered. "However, this news cannot wait. It is potentially the turning point of the war."

Stephen had heard that before. Still, he thought to himself that hope springs forever, even if sleep must end.

The General lead a growing entourage across the palace's Northern lawn. Dew collected across Stephen's royal slippers. A mild spell prevented it from dampening his feet. He only wished they were his actual shoe size. Abdura was in a war economy, and he had to make due with a lot of his predecessor's clothes. He had drawn the line at royal boxer shorts. They came to a refrigeration truck parked in the driveway. One of the twenty heavily armed guards unbolted the rear doors at Bloomengardt's nod.

"We used this truck as camouflage, sire, but its cool interior proved an asset in transporting the living cargo."

"Living?"

"Yes, in a manner of interpretation."

The truck doors swung open. Inside the icy compartment snarled and a chained and shivering monstrosity. It looked much like a progression of Mythilda's mutations. It was smaller than a full-fledged demon, and still obviously a young man in torn fatigues having suffered grotesque, emerald alterations. Bloomengardt paid no attention to the growling captive as he spoke to Stephen.

"Your highness, you directed Solerno and Sonenberg to find if a demon could be changed back into a maiden. Although male," Bloomengardt looked at the shivering captive to check his facts. "This creature is at half-way stage. We wish to use him in those experiments. However, that is not covered in the War Accords, so we need your sanction."

"That is not covered, but bombing cities is?"

"Yes, sire. We need to move quickly, sire."

"Of course." Stephen moved closer to the rear of the truck, and, to the surprise of his entourage, spoke to the demonic soldier. "Excuse me. I'm King Stephen of Abdura—"

"And I am a living terror! The death of you all!" The creature howled.

"Actually, you're chained and freezing. So, not much of a threat. I'd like to know if you wish to stay that way."

"No," it replied. "I'd really like a blanket and a cup of tea, if you have one."

"I do. But the chains will stay on. And what I meant was, do you wish to stay a demon, or would you like to be a man again?"

"Yes!" it shrieked "I didn't want to be a demonic soldier to start!"

"Then, why are you?"

"Well, it seemed like the right thing to do. Everyone in the country was doing it. Even the Queen!"

"I see," Stephen nodded. "Do you like your Queen?"

"Really? No. I didn't vote for her. Too right wing."

"Hmm. Do you think the other people in your army would welcome being reverted back to human?"

"Yes! These scales itch far more than the sauro-wool uniforms." The creature rubbed against his chains.

"Okay. I'll see what I can do."

The creature howled again. Stephen took it as gratitude. He stepped back and soldiers slammed the doors shut.

"We will immediately take him to Solerno and Sonenberg." Bloomengardt beamed and flashed a rare smile.

"See if you can get him a blanket and tea, once you get there. No point in not being civil."

"Ah, yes, sire."

Breton pushed ahead to face Bloomengardt and Stephen. "If this cure works, how do we administer it without simply turning these demon soldiers back into normal troops who still serve Pangea?"

"Well," Stephen rubbed his eyes. "We can release a few successfully, and I do mean successfully treated soldiers. They can show Abdura has such power to help them all. I would expect a mass defection."

"That was essentially my plan, sire." Bloomengardt bowed his head.

"Well then, General, start it as soon as possible." Stephen smiled. Mythilda's antagonism had stirred him. Suddenly, their past inspired him. "Let's also let it be known that if you defect, you'll have a job here in Abdura."

"A job, sire?" Bloomengardt joined Breton to look quizzically at their king.

"Trust me, gentlemen. Or, at least, just do it. Please."

One week later, and Stephen eagerly rose from bed to speak with Solerno and Sonenberg through the communications parlor. Although, Stephen was glad that, so far, their lab had stayed intact. Both men were visible on the king's screen. Behind them sat a young man, obviously uncomfortable to be only wearing a hospital gown. Stephen recognized the former demon soldier even without green eyes, scales, and looking a bit thinner.

"Our efforts are a success, your highness!" Solerno beamed, and pointed to the young man behind him. "Our guest is cured, and quite well."

"He has an annoying habit of urinating frequently." Sonenberg added.

"Is that a side effect of the treatment?" Stephen asked.

"No, sire." Solerno answered. "It is because he drinks rather a lot of tea. Evidently it tastes better here than in Pangea."

"I see, Professor. You're confident the treatment can be duplicated?"

"Yes! And the serum requires no refrigeration!" Solerno looked overjoyed.

"We're thinking of administering it in tea," Sonenberg added. "But that might make them all—"

"We already have a plan for mass manufacture, sire." Solerno interrupted and earned an arm swat by his elder colleague.

"Do you drink a lot of tea, King Stephen?" Sonenberg asked, and peered closely into the camera.

"No, Professor. I'm partial to coffee."

"Even worse," the elder professor shook his head.

"I know, Professor. I used to be a plumber."

In the weeks since the successful cure of the demonic soldier, the war had put new pressures on the Interior. Breton joined the military briefing. Stephen noted that he was the only one not wearing something cast from metal, or shiny. Other than his hair.

"I've requested to speak first, your highness." Breton began. "I'm afraid we have something of an issue involving the defection of demonic soldiers."

"Actually, they're not quite demons." Sonenberg interjected. "For one thing they don't breathe fire."

"I certainly hope the cure is still working." Stephen feared the reply.

"Yes, sire!" Solerno exclaimed, and glared suspiciously at Breton. "It must certainly be a bureaucratic problem."

"The cure is working well, sire." Breton continued.

"The enemy is defecting in droves. The defectors are remarkably well behaved for, ah, if not demons, then simply, for weirdly mutated enemy soldiers.

"Our problem is that we cannot cure and release the Pangeans fast enough. There is tremendous overcrowding of our prison camps, and we are hard pressed to find places in the job market to honor your promise of employment, sire."

"Well, start with the juggernaut plants." Stephen said. "That will ease the demand on conscripts being diverted to industry."

"Can we trust them in our weapons factories, sire?"

"I assume it will depend on the benefits package. We're already offering good health coverage. Dental, too." Stephen lapsed into thought. "If we could launch demons in missiles that ultimately caused this plague, could we cure it that way?"

The room was silent. The faint buzz of electric lamps seemed to become louder.

"What I mean is, could the serum be delivered through a missile burst?"

66

Solerno's face went through a gymnastic display as the idea cartwheeled through his brain.

"Well, sire," Solerno's face slowed its motions. "If demons come from maidens, why can't a cure fall from the sky?"

"How artistic, Professor." Stephen said. "See what you can do."

"Quickly, please." Breton added.

The roar subsided inside the command suite as rocket motors pushed the serum-filled warheads high above the silos. Bloomengardt was happy to use his new missiles beyond the testing range. Solerno and Sonenberg were eager to see their airburst serum tested over so great an area. It had worked as an aerosol in the prison camps, but this was an epic application. Stephen secretly hoped this strike would eliminate hostilities once and for all, and without leveling a single building. He was also glad the deafening roar of the missile launch was over, and disappointed the ringing in his ears had returned.

Stephen's scalp began tightening before he entered the briefing room for an emergency meeting. Breton, Bloomengardt, Ashland, Solerno, and Sonenberg all stood with serious expressions that elevated the tension. Stephen was certain the news was grim. Instead, he found the intelligence related to him utterly laughable. He imagined his belligerent opponent, enemy queen, and ex-wife seeing the aftermath of the serum-missile strikes. His idea had worked. Perhaps too well. He felt a great sense of mirth rise within himself.

"So, now--" Stephen drew out each syllable to buy time and focus. "They've, ah, they've become maidens." He suppressed a giggle, but his voice reached a high pitch. "You mean all of them?"

"Yes, sire." Bloomengardt answered. "The entire population of Pangea has become young, and we assume pure, women."

A series of chuckles slowly rose within Stephen. Then laughter seized control of him completely. He fell and rolled in spasms of manic joy. The assembled advisors stared with mouths agape as their king contorted before them. Stephen regained self-control when he saw Sonenberg begin fumbling in his pocket.

"I'm all right," Stephen wheezed. He realized he had probably shattered what respected he had gained as king, but he didn't care. For once his forehead was completely relaxed. "My headache is gone! I think I've had it for months. Well, another unknown side-effect to your serum, Professors."

"Actually, that could be caused by the lack of oxygen while you—" Solerno began.

"I was kidding, Professor." Stephen rubbed his aching gut and stood. "Now, do you have an idea of how long this will last?"

"Permanently." Sonenberg replied.

He finally withdrew a small atomizer from his pocket and aimed it at Stephen. The younger Solerno snatched it away in horror before a drop hit the spout. Solerno showed the label to the indignant Sonenberg, whose face then also flashed with shock. He shrugged and gazed up in feigned innocence while taking a step and away from the atomizer in Solerno's hand.

"We're not sure if it was the intensity of the dose, or how we reformulated the serum for warhead delivery," Solerno said while hiding the atomizer behind him. "The roots of our research were done with actual demon tissue, not the more mild mutates."

"The artillery shell delivery has had the same effects at the front, sire." Ashland reported. "The enemy soldiers, all of whom had been mutated, have become young maidens. Many of our male soldiers who were due for leave are now requesting to remain at the front."

The last comment caused a renewed burst of chuckling from Stephen.

"Despite the odd situation, we've not pulled back." Ashland added innocently. "Our frontline units want to keep advancing. All positions can push forward."

Stephen clutched his mouth closed.

"Sire," Bloomengardt waited for Stephen to be calm. "I feel this could be an enemy trick, to lull us into a state of—" Bloomengardt stopped himself upon seeing Ashland's own growing smile.

"With all due respect," Ashland said. "You really need to go to the front. I'm certain we'd have seen any deceitful actions by now. We've entered the Pangean frontier with no resistance. Encounters between forces have been respectful. The Pangean leadership has broken down. There is no one urging their army to attack. The new state of being has made most, if not all Pangeans, reconsider life in general, General."

"I imagine that if you had been an old man, a renewed life is worth preserving." Stephen mused. "Even if it's now life as a young woman."

"Most Pangeans are glad the hostilities have stopped." Ashland added. "Honestly, so am I."

"I guess the war is over." Solerno voiced Stephen's hope.

"General Ashland," Stephen said in full control. "I assume my ex-wife is now not only unemployed, but on the run. Perhaps at sea. So when you get to the Pangean capital, find some maidens that were once jurists and legislators. Perhaps we can formalize a treaty."

"I'll get there soon, sire!" Ashland's teeth shone as an ivory beacon.

There were few clauses contested in the peace treaty. Strangely enough, native Pangeans did not like fish all that much to start with. Fishing just seemed like a good thing to do if the neighbors were doing it. That, and a certain former queen had owned a boat building company. The ink of Stephen's treaty signature was hardly dry when Breton entered Stephen's office, more dour than usual.

"The need for juggernauts has plummeted." Breton's voice was muffled by a stack of parchments and the new type of paper that tried to escape the filing cabinets.

Stephen waved away his aides, and peered around the stack to find Breton.

"I would think that's a good thing." Stephen said, finally in line of sight with Breton.

"Only in terms of the war, sire. We already have a massive surplus of munitions. With the war is over, the weapons factories are shutting down. Thanks to your promise of a job to all defectors, we face unprecedented unemployment in the swollen Abduran population."

"Surely many of the defectors will want to go home."

"No. Most Pangean men are afraid to return to their former country."

"They fear becoming dates for our male troops, I take it." Stephen chuckled.

"At least those troops have a job, for as long as we can pay them." Breton said, almost defiantly. "The ultimate result of your policies has reduced our proud nation to a country of paupers."

"Ultimately, Breton, I ended the war. Peace should have it rewards. Unless wrestling with demons is your secret vocation?"

"No, sire." Breton replied slightly bowing before Stephen's glare. "But the crisis we face now is not one of missiles, armored weapons, demons, and serums."

Stephen was surprised he could say that with a dismissive tone.

"It's the economy, your highness. I'm afraid I must call together the quorum and discuss a new lottery."

Stephen could see the reverberations from his fit of laughter. However, he was still glad for having it. "You will indeed need to do so, Breton."

Stephen pushed a drafted document slowly creeping across his desk towards Breton.

"I am resigning as king."

"That's impossible."

"No. I'm the king, and I say it is possible. Consider it my last official act."

"It will certainly be a precedent." Breton flexed his cheeks beneath his widening eyelids.

Stephen wondered of his surprise was from the document or its own locomotion.

"It may be a minority view, but I feel I did well for our nation. True, we face new challenges, but when don't we? I was just getting good at being me when I became king. Odd thing, it was being a ruler of other people that made me want to be in control of my own life. It's the best freedom I can imagine."

"Interesting. May I ask what you intend to do now?"

"I think I'll volunteer for the Reconstruction Corps we've sent to Pangea. I was once good with a wrench. And, anyway, they're actually looking to hire people."

"You want to help rebuild the country you tried to blow up?"

"I wanted to end the war. It took a while, but I did. You must admit, using a missile as a vaccine needle was a novel idea."

Breton's only response was a squint and flex of his left cheek.

"You could argue I did more to change Pangea than Abdura."

Stephen smiled. Breton did not.

"Perhaps you should visit to the Royal Psychiatrist, your highness. While you still can."

"Thank you for your concern, but I don't think irony is a medical condition. I'm just going to grab my wrenches instead. Perhaps the former male king of Abdura moving to Pangea will inspire other men to follow. That would reduce the one-sided population problem."

Breton nodded affirmation.

Stephen imagined waves of people of one country flowing into the other and vice versa. After a time, there might just be a single nation and planet named Pan-Abdura. It sounded better than Portis.

"I'll fetch your tool box." Breton finally smiled.

The ride was nearly tolerable. The 'nauts improved suspension eased the jarring impacts. Still, Stephen thought, the metal beasts made lousy taxis. At least the charmed air fresheners masked some of the stench. Yet, they were still noisy and uncomfortable. The virtue of the rugged machines was low cost and ample spare parts. They were a good deal for the burgeoning frontier transit companies. Roads were still being laid between the countries. Stephen hoped they would be finished, soon.

The former Abduran king walked the Pangean city streets with combed hair, no fanfare, no mantelet, and few worries. There were maidens everywhere, doing every job in the shattered remains of buildings, in tents, and huts. Stephen wondered what some of them had been before his missiles exploded over the city. He decided he needed a vacation from thinking. He seemed a popular subject for stares and smiles. He smiled himself.

Stephen had lied to Breton. His last official act was not merely resigning, but also appointing his daughter to succeed him. There was no restriction from doing so. No king had ever done it before Stephen. Now Merry Ann was a young, idealistic queen. Stephen had no doubt she'd govern better than her parents had. She would have at least three, identical advisors she could trust. And she had always been partial to birds, even gigantic, teal ones.

"Excuse me," A young brunette women left the scorched doorway of a nearly intact apartment house. "You're with the rebuilding corps?"

Stephen's utility suit and tool box answered for him. "How can I help you?"

"How can't you?" She sighed.

"I'm Stephen. And I'll do what I can. It's my new job."

72

"What did you do during the war?" The woman's curiosity was pointed, as was her cautious gaze.

"Well," Stephen paused. "I suffered a headache, fought with my wife, and argued with my daughter."

"Hmm. Not so exciting." Her posture relaxed.

"You don't know my family." Stephen smiled.

"I'm Cegride. I have a backed-up sink in my apartment's kitchen. I can't get to the clog. Can you help fix it?"

"It's why I'm here."

Cegride returned his smile and opened the door. Stephen found the young Cegride quite attractive, and an odd feeling overtook him.

"Are you partial to birds, Cegride?"

"Not really. Why?"

Stephen felt relived. "Just making conversation. Now, where is your sink?"

"The kitchen. Naturally." Cegride answered.

Stephen followed her into the building. His brow was completely at ease.

CICADA

Dust rolled tall and heavy over the boardwalk. The dying glare of the evening sun appeared to push the flanks of amber clouds inside Riley's saloon. It was more desert to sweep out and collect between the creaking planks. Sally didn't mind. It would never be her job to sweep. She stayed clear of the falling dust, and watched it carefully to see if it moved on its own. Old Chief just sat silently at his table and looked forward. He was never moved by strange movements, loud music, or anything else. Sometimes he would snuffle his great, craggy nose. The soundtrack of his snuffle was just slightly out of step with his projection. Hardly anyone but Sally noticed. Even in these modern days of the 1800s, most travelers through the slatted, spring-hinged doors never thought reality could also part, swing open and let anything come through. But that it did, and often, in Cicada.

All anyone needed to see was the art on Riley's walls to know the land out West was much weirder than its descriptions back East. Riley especially liked artists in the future. He felt a work was worth more if the artist wasn't born yet. Sally was partial to the painting by that Norwegian, Munch. Sometimes she grabbed her cheeks like the ghostly person on the bridge in a silent wail. She saw many people do the same during the Shifts. People adjust, though. Most times.

Cicada's population stayed just slightly under the number of available houses, boarding rooms, and jail cells. It was enough people to support Riley's businesses, along with the passers by. Now and again newcomers would replace the disappeared. People from Indian nations, settlers, cowboys and rustlers would come in. Then something would happen and they would have to stay. Either madness or something deep inside their minds compelled they settle here. Rare times it was the desire to keep seeing all the weirdness and such. Sally pondered if such yearning was the same thing as madness.

Sally thought about such distinctions, and if she could ever be sure what was real. Her own mind was manufactured. Still, she felt her fabricated eyes were better than others at deciding when nature slipped a step. Sally functioned with more precision than the oddly bright jukebox, and Old Chief's timing processor. Sally had been switched on for so long that entropy had worn away the predilections of her programming. Most of them, at least.

It was not that Sally had profound thoughts. That's what she told herself. She was still a saloon girl. Yet the hard luck story of falling from grace and abduction from the convent now sounded, well, artificial. Her supposed life's tale had been spun just as the fine, tall glasses under the bar. Those fancy glasses were seldom used, unlike Sally. Sally never liked to touch glass, or drink really. Perhaps, this was because part of her had been born out of something much like a bottle. She grew tired of touch in general. But she was still a saloon girl. Sally could handle any number of customers during day and night, and never tire nor need time to heal. Riley seemed like a good man. He talked to Sally like a real person. Why would he have bought a slave? He likely never thought Sally would come to ask such questions. Riley never had any good answers, and always a lot of work to do.

When the wind curled outside and made a little wail, Sally would slowly step from the bar to look warily down the rutted, dirt street. When sunlight was a weak curtain of pink or orange over the emerging night, Riley went to light the lamps outside. He used a thousand automatic things in his saloon, like Sally. Yet he still suffered with sulfur matches and oil lanterns over the boardwalk. Sally always hoped the wailing would die. On those quiet nights the Whirl never came to town. Other nights, her hope died like the spur of flame on Riley's matches in the breeze.

Most folk, those of the flesh and otherwise, acted kindly in their first minute or two after coming through the saloon doors. This was especially true of those stepping in for the first time. Then, some would notice the weird paintings as the first bit of odd. Most wearing suits and bowler hats stopped smiling. They drank their liquor quickly, but slow enough to wonder if the glass held anything as strange as the paintings and odd, bright objects hung here and there.

Whirl of the Darkness didn't need Shift, horse, or coach to come to town. The wind would spin and sag, laden with dust colored more darkly than the earth around town. The whirlwind would split, and out he would walk. Like many people and other things, the Whirl adapted to Cicada. In the first moments when the Whirl came to town, he acted like a gentleman. But unlike a man, the Whirl couldn't be put off by strangeness on the wall. He looked like the nightmare of the muse that inspired them all: surreal; terrible; sad destiny draped in black. Perhaps more odd, the Whirl had desires like any man. And Sally was always there. She tired of the sensation of swirling soot like an abrasive spinning over her. Sand and soot didn't sweat. Whirl of the Darkness, though, left a dank sheen like the blood of a sage bush if you snapped a thick branch deep. But he never pulled her hair. Sally took what small comfort there was when the Whirl left his gold on the bar.

Gold could bring some little comfort itself. Riley ordered wares from a catalogue that floated like a globe in the air. Riley kept his orders within a hundred years past or future. Shipping costs got more expensive beyond that. One day he let Sally order something for herself. Riley looked at her order befuddled, and said it was a waste of money. Stuff like snake oil never worked. Sally looked at Riley and laughed. This was Cicada, after all.

Riley assumed Sally would've ordered something soft or pretty. Sally countered that maybe it would be. The advertisement said Doctor Morpho's Special Matter could be anything, so long as he received proper thanks as described in directions, and the order was postpaid. And it wasn't half as much as the new beer mugs. Sally wondered what those would sound like smashed against the head of a rustler or cowboy.

They wouldn't break, Riley told her. About the customer's skull, Riley only shrugged.

As a business man, Riley tried to keep profits up and prices fair. The saloon was all he had left. Sally knew he could never go back home to Philadelphia. Cicada was home, weird as it was. Maybe its Shifts and special properties made Riley think his former life was unreal. He ran his bar well enough, but Sally silently questioned some things. While sitting with Old Chief she realized he should be an outdoor display. He was designed to look down the road or to the horizon, not just at the wall opposite him. He was likely meant to look over at the saloon from afar as an advertisement draped in local color. But everyone knew where the saloon was, and Riley's prices seemed reasonable to most everything that came through the doors.

Later on, Dr. Morpho's package came. Sally carefully unfolded the violet foil wrapper. Inside the small paper box rested a little blue bottle no longer than her pinky finger. Beneath it was the long, blue nugget of Special Matter. Each of its lustrous, five-sides reflected the saloon light. Its odor was strong. Sally could smell it through the scents of spilled spirits, dust, ozone and tobacco that wafted through Riley's place. It smelled old and sweet like the fragrance of a fossilized chrysanthemum. Smaller pieces of the metal mounded up beside it. Sally unfolded the directions, careful to let the blue dust in the creases fall into the box. She attentively read the directions, but fretted on how to get the time to do the ritual. Riley wanted her on the saloon floor when she wasn't with a customer or two.

Her answer walked in with two friends. Sally gladly took the cowboy upstairs. She had never struck anyone before, and wondered if the blow would be hard enough to knock the nervous young man unconscious. Her blushing client bounced off the wall. Outside ears would think it was just another rough customer. Luckily the chants were much like she carried on anyway. She signed the warranty card and placed it beside the wash basin and pitcher to mail. The Special Matter relaxed and coolly melted into a small puddle of sapphire mercury across the violet foil. Sally poured her curious purchase into the little blue bottle. Now, whenever she wished, smashing the bottle would transform its contents into her thoughts incarnate. Or so said the pamphlet. Sally tied a ribbon around the small blue bottle and hung it from the mirror. She stripped the gun and clothes from the grimy young man, and slapped him gently to hasten his waking.

The bottle hung from Sally's neck between her corset and dress so it wouldn't touch her skin. It remained there long enough for Riley and a few regulars to grow weary of teasing Sally about her dubious purchase. The night was quiet, cold and dark when the rustlers came in. There were four. Each was sweaty from trail fever, dirty, and there wasn't a white tooth among them. They all looked at Sally with the usual gaze over her body, and little interest in what she said. Maybe these men could entertain her for a change. Sally tossed the little blue bottle down as they approached her. It made little noise shattering. The sapphire mercury splattered across the beaten wood floor. Nothing happened.

The lead rustler picked Sally up and pulled at the lace frill of her dress with his yellowed teeth. Startled cuss words exploded behind him and his stench. The lead rustler didn't notice nor care. Then came the sound of gun metal pulled fast against leather. The rumble of overturning glasses and chairs followed. The loud staccato of firing six-guns obliterated all other noise. One set of guns started faster and ended after the violent jumble of irregular booms and hammers hitting dud cartridges.

The lead rustler dropped Sally and spun to the violence with hands on gun handles. Sally hit the table and tumbled through Old Chief. The rustler froze upon seeing the smoking ends of two silver pistols that Sally's freshly made gunslinger pointed at him. The face of her new protector was a ghostly, bending mask of brushstrokes locked in an anguished scream.

In contrast, his eyes glared purposefully at the rustler. Still, Mr. Munch would have easily recognized him. The strange Gunslinger slid his pistols back into their ornate holsters.

The odd appearances of his opponent only delayed the rustler's malignant bravado. His arms lurched up and snaked at his weird target. The Gunslinger's barrels jumped back up swifter than even the hammer click of the rustler's guns. Two silver Colts made a single, loud boom. The bullets ripped the last rustler off his boot heels. He struck the plank floor with a heavy thud.

Even the newer metal cartridges left a heavy haze of sulfur smoke after firing. It seemed to blend with Sally's sudden champion. The Gunslinger stood tall and broad shouldered. His boots and holsters were tamped with a matching pattern. A gambler's vest, complete with extra aces, stretched over his rugged build. Ironically, the same wavy strokes of paint creating his ghostly face also made his body. The Gunslinger was a patchwork of the unconscious impressions of Sally's surroundings because she didn't think to describe him when making her wish. Now that Sally had made something of her own, she suddenly grasped the usefulness, rather the importance of imagination, even though its progeny had surrounded her for so long.

Sally's creation was less important to Riley. Vexing him was what to do with the rustled cattle just outside town. They were no doubt watched over by partners of the dead men that left oozed blood stains on his floorboards. The men watching the cattle would want their turn in town. If those men learned their partners had been gunned down, they might stampede the herd through Cicada. Who knows what might happen, then. It would be a shame to see the cattle suffer. On the morning, the Gunslinger went out and put an end to further speculations. Evidently, the other rustlers were also bad tempered.

The town let the cattle graze where they could outside town. Maybe their true owner would find and collect them.

Sally now spent most nights seated with Old Chief, and the Gunslinger. Riley wondered how this chimera of six-gun Expressionism would affect business. Even the locals found no interest in Sally now she had a man of her own, or something like a man. Not that he did anything untoward to local folk. People would relax more when he learned to speak. Riley worried that his voice would match his expression.

Sally remained proud. She had made him, and she undertook his upkeep much like a mother with a new cub. Everyone, especially Riley, knew his skill with his guns gave Sally a different standing in town. Most began to except the new order of things. And then Whirl of the Darkness came back to town.

When the wind blew and scratched at the saloon doors, everyone knew he was him fixing to come. At the East end of town, a wind howled like a coyote shot with an arrow just off the mark. Outside, the splitting whirlwind wailed. The sound was as if someone desperate tried to use a buffalo hide to muffle thunder. All eyes saw the darkening of the night. Sally stood rigidly at the bar when the Whirl entered. He moved toward her expecting the same treatment as always. This time Sally moved away and turned her back. The Whirl followed, drawing cold from somewhere far outside. The Gunslinger stood, hands on guns, and faced up with the Whirl. No one had ever looked directly at the Whirl before, except Sally.

There was no reason the Whirl would notice a new towner like the Gunslinger, but there was no ignoring his intentions. A low howl grew louder. Everyone's teeth felt the vibration as it grew louder still. The bar visibly vibrated, and then splinters and brass ripped right out of it. The shards spun and flew all over the saloon. The Gunslinger began to scream, too. The two banshees stood locked in a sonic brawl that drove most people out holding their ears and dodging more and more shards cracking free.

Whirl of the Darkness expanded. The images and cries of a thousand people caught and crushed in desert whirlwinds flashed and wailed like mangled shadows from his insides. The skin and leather of the Gunslinger began to bur away. His screams were of pain, now. He fell and struck the wall as if gravity confused its direction. Paintings of Samaras and Ernst offered little to soften his collision. The Gunslinger's jaws became exposed. Pieces of Special Matter flew from his bone like nuggets out of a river bank. There wasn't any blood, just a blue haze caught in the maelstrom like an unraveling ghost.

Her creation was dying. Sally attempted to offer herself to the Whirl. Riley held her back out of the same paternal instinct that Sally felt for the Gunslinger screaming against the wall. They struggled amid the swirling chaos. Sally stopped fighting Riley, and focused on the Gunslinger's torture. She had brought him into this bizarre world of Cicada. He had changed her life in a good way. If the Whirl won this duel, Sally's would again be the only saloon girl in town. Her resentment surfaced in her own screams. If the Gunslinger was to die, then let her go with him. Better yet, she thought, let the darkness die and they live.

Slowly, the Gunslinger rose. He closed his mouth and fought to step from the wall back to the saloon floor. He braced himself against the Whirl's onslaught, and drew his Colts. The Whirl was gunned down in front of the bar like so many other black figures in saloons across the West. There was a thud. The maelstrom lost its force and the debris began to clatter across the saloon. A strange stain seeped between the planks. Sulfur combined with some awful stench that drifted across the bar and died itself. The room fell silent. There was much more for Riley to sweep out now.

Riley never finished fixing-up the saloon. In that instinctive moment of trying to protect Sally, he realized life, whatever its shape or origin, was worth more than being an asset in a saloon. The search for his own freedom had spurred his travel out West long ago. The Pacific Ocean was still farther West, and farther still from Philadelphia. Riley and a few speculators in town drove off with the rustled cattle to see if the ground was more solid closer to the sea. The town was fairly certain they made it past the city limits.

Sally made some breakthroughs of her own. She began to realize when watching the Gunslinger step from the wall and assert himself over the Whirl, that the mind was the engine driving the weird Shifts of Cicada. That fight ended the way she imagined it should, after all. Her Gunslinger lived and the Whirl died. The saloon's repairs came quicker than most expected. The new owner made some changes in the decor to suit her own developing tastes. Sally decided she liked Realism. It was an ironic motif chosen to contrast with the outside. Some of the regulars complained about the higher price of whisky. But Sally's was the only saloon in town. In Cicada, it was likely to remain that way.

The Gunslinger healed, too. He stayed in the back room playing cards with the more trustworthy locals. A silver star of authority replaced his extra aces. Old Chief now sat on the new bench out front, and looked towards the horizon at day. At night he gazed at the moon, when it was around. No real thoughts clouded his projected head. On quiet mornings, Sally would join him and think for both of them. The bar was Sally's place now. She owned it, as well as the future and the past, and all the weird places in between. The shape and attitude of her customers didn't matter anymore. Sally could welcome or refuse service to anyone. It didn't pay to dispute the proprietor when the very air and dust curled on the edges of her smile.

THE LAST OCTOBER NIGHT

The gathering was over. Goblins and demons reverted back to myth with their faces cast across the couch and carpet. One by one they enjoyed fleeting resurrection as each mask passed over the cherubic face that emerged from the hallway shadows. Meg was glad she wasn't asleep. Eating a vast amount of Halloween candy helped her young mind stay awake. Meg's personal magic also aided her consciousness, and more. She felt its power grow, even as a child. Tonight it was very strong.

Meg crept passed her father who stood outside the opened front door. His breath curled in the cold night air as he waved good-bye to party guests. Meg had always sensed he loved her through a delicate sadness. Like most people, he was missing the special magnetism and the extra senses that came with it. Meg could hear her mother farther outside speaking to departing friends. She was distracted. That was good. Meg could act, at last. In her demon disguise she climbed a chair beside the dining table. Sadly, the bowl held only unsavory black jellybeans and sickly-sweet sugar dust. Her plan had failed.

Meg tossed her mask aside. The reflection on the polished table of the old, ornate cabinet caught her attention. She studied the hand-carved woodland design on its doors. For a moment she became lost in the carved relief of trees. The top compartment was an object of occasional wonder for her. Inside her parents kept things they pretended had no interest for little girls. However, Meg knew its contents would someday be hers. From the table's edge she could reach the cabinet's doors. They seemed to glide open with welcoming silence. Inside the compartment were books. All were too heavy to budge, except one. Like the cabinet doors, the book seemed to glide to her with little effort on her part.

Meg frowned at the swirling letters handwritten on the thick, crinkling pages. Yet, somehow her mind found the writer's voice. It was a man's voice, but certainly not her father. She felt the voice touch the force inside her. The words spoke directly to Meg, and she eagerly read on. Meg's heart beat faster. Her magic grew stronger. The lyric words drew a story of a dragon and a little girl. Meg knew she was that girl. Only she could set the dragon free to soar into this last, cold October night.

A storm gathered. Wind drove frigid mist and leaves together with littered wrappers across the darkened suburban landscape. Car exhaust mingled with the cloying odors of fast-food. The scents offended the man walking across the empty, dim parking lot. His heavy boots severed oil rainbows in shallow puddles. In the aging storefronts ahead of him, a smile appeared in darkness. It somehow escaped the supermarket sign's bleaching glare. Like a shadow peeled from a wall, the floating smile emerged. The grin attached to a man dressed in black. He stood to greet the other man who arrived by the more mundane method of walking.

Heavy boots met the storefront curb. The walker's breath chilled into a white veil before him. Mist drops glistened in his thick, brown beard in the artificial light. In contrast, the smiling man who stepped from shadow slipped the weather's effects. Long, saffron hair moved only when he did, untouched by the wind. His fine features appeared crafted from translucent porcelain.

"And here we are, called out again, William." The man dressed in shadows said.

"Just as the seasons return, Michael. Although the places of our hidden acts change, as does the Earth," William said. He stood beside the shadowed Michael, but the location fascinated him more than his strange companion. "This place is an appropriate motif for Earth's present. A polluted field of asphalt next to a condemned forest."

"It is like you to find an allegory out of chance." Michael replied.

Now William smiled, darkly. He looked up at the rolling clouds. Reflected city light colored them purple. Thunder sounded over houses nearby, and rumbled towards him.

Meg awoke with a jolt.

"And what are you doing, my little Meg?" Her father asked. He pushed his eyeglasses up towards his eyes to better focus on her.

Meg had become very tired after finishing the dragon story. Her father looked down at her sternly. Meg rubbed her eyes to delay answering. She would wait for her mother before trying to explain her obvious guilt.

"Meg?" Her mother said sharply as she entered the house. Meg: the name her mother chose carefully. It was simple, feminine, but strong. Most of all, it was free of hidden meanings and connotations potentially heaped upon the child. It would be a benign shield in her childhood, for as long as that could last.

Meg watched sheepishly as her parents rigid stares moved from her to the opened cabinet and transformed into expressions of dreadful surprise. Her father looked back at Meg and snatched up the book she had found.

"Jennifer, where did this come from?" He asked.

"I don't know," Jennifer said quietly to her husband, Peter. She took the book from him and looked at it briefly, before returning her gaze to Meg.

Meg saw a strange quality in her mother's expression. Surprise and perhaps fear danced in her blue-black eyes. Meg knew her mother could sense the stronger magic flourishing inside her, and felt as though she should hide it. However it wasn't something she could shove under a pillow. Her father observed them quietly. His face held that familiar look each time he looked at Meg. He always flashed a quick smile over it, but Meg knew there was something about her that troubled him. His attempts to disguise the emotion only made it obvious.

"He was here, wasn't he?" Peter said.

Jennifer remained silent, but a volume of unspoken words raced between them. The wound Meg's father covered with his quick smiles opened again. Meg looked at the book and understood the man her father refused to name was its author. Her mother read its pages with growing concern. Her father looked back at Meg. This time the smile faded. Meg felt the reaction caused by this other man. It smoldered beyond her own reflection in her father's eyeglasses.

Lightning flashed. Multiple images of William reflected across the glass storefronts as thunder rolled like manic, baritone laughter. The storm grew stronger.

"Do you ever wonder for what purpose things happen?" William asked. "Is there something other than Magic's aberrations we must redress? Is something else at work?"

"Magic has no aberrations, itself." Michael answered. "Other forces cause rips in the ether, tatters to mend. That is why I exist. So, mine is not to reason why. I simply do, for I cannot die."

"Paraphrased clichés created by someone who was never truly born." William observed. "Can apocalypse be far away?"

"I hope not," Michael countered. "I like my job."

"Wouldn't you rather be able to act from your own will, as a free man?"

"I am not truly a man, William," Michael replied. He assumed a female appearance. "And who among us is truly free? I am familiar with the work of Ivan Pavlov and B.F. Skinner. I concur that human learning and behavior are determined by environmental forces, rather than inherent intelligence. So can it be different for Magic? Its own mind flows from all other minds bound by environmental chains."

"Your comments both elate and disappoint me, Michael." William suddenly stopped before the woods. "I had expected you to be a fiercer champion of human life."

86

"I leave that to the living," Michael said, carefully observing William's change in tone.

"Then, you have failed."

Meg sat at Jennifer's feet happily drawing with colored pencils. Her talent was another gift shared with Jennifer. Peter paced nervously as Jennifer sat and analyzed the mysterious book. He looked at Meg's art and stopped. Its intensity of alternating colors mesmerized him. He broke free with a shudder.

"What has that monster done to our daughter?" Peter spouted to Jennifer.

"He is no monster, Peter." Jennifer answered.

Her voice was an emotional balm. He felt at peace. She made that small, simple smile that belied her strength. That quality drew Peter to her. She awakened in him sensations he doubted anyone had felt before. That was before Jennifer revealed her other gifts, and why his love remained unchanged when his wife said she wanted to bear a child. Not his child, not yet. Jennifer told him this child would be more special than herself. The good it would bring was worth their possible pain. He remembered believing that. Or was that Jennifer's memory? At times he couldn't be sure. He was certain he never wanted to lose Jennifer. Whatever she loved, he would welcome into his life.

"Why did he need Meg?" Peter asked. "I know this is all about Magic, or the ethereal stuff that people like me can't touch. By why Meg?"

"You know why." Jennifer answered. "Meg is the union of two of the three souls that interact with Magic. It makes her very powerful."

"Like this chump who invaded our home tonight, unseen." Peter sneered.

"Be cautious, Peter. He is one form. To put it simply, he is an Actor. There are also Reactors, and Agents. Actors are like William, Meg's—" she halted. "The other biological donor. Actors interact directly with Magic. They set spells in motion. They can alter reality. But their influence is limited by the extent of their own power, and, if necessary, by Reactors and Agents."

"Like you?" Peter said.

"Yes. I'm a Reactor. I'm empathic. I can alter spells only by altering the minds of Actors."

"And William is a powerful Actor." Peter looked downward and sighed.

"Perhaps the most powerful. We saw our union as a means to create an even stronger, human soul that could employ magic, but not be bound by it. We imagined such a child would grow up to guide and protect all humanity. At least I did."

Jennifer slumped in her chair. Her outlook darkened like Peter's mood.

"So William is changing the rules." Peter said.

"Yes. But even he must answer to Magic and the judgment of the rest of us. Whatever he has done must by now be seen by at least one Agent, by now."

"You think the agent will help you?" Peter asked.

"Yes. If William's plans are harmful to life. But even they need help from people like me to alter events. Sometimes their understanding is limited. They aren't really human, but aspects of magic sent to interact with us. They didn't exist until life evolved intelligent thought."

"But they're good guys. Right?" Peter asked with his eyebrows raised over his glasses.

"As good as a battery." Jennifer answered.

"Huh?" Peter pushed his glasses back.

"They represent power. A power beyond this plane. Power that we other two kinds can tap." Jennifer drew a deep breath and dreaded hearing her own words that followed. "But that power will act for its best interests. Agents interact with this plane through people like William and me. But they will do so only if it helps Magic. It's self preserving."

"Sounds more like Magic is self-serving!" Peter snapped.

Meg glanced up at Peter for a moment.

"Watch what you say," Jennifer cautioned. "But, yes, that's true."

"Great." Peter resumed his pacing.

"Let me decipher his plan. William has always acted to save Earth, to save life. The situation tonight must been very dire, and done in ebbing time."

"But he had time to write and plant the book."

"This might have been an emergency plan. He always liked to work out all possible details. There aren't many variables he hasn't encountered." Jennifer closed the book and seemed to look at something, or someone, in the distance.

Peter tensed again. He knelt beside Meg, who had remained quiet to watch and learn.

"Meg," Peter asked in as gentle a voice as he could muster. "Did you see anyone tonight you didn't know? Did someone visit you?"

"Someone was in the book." Meg answered.

"Do you understand what happens in the story?" Jennifer asked.

"Yes," Meg replied happily. "I set the dragon free."

"When?" Jennifer asked. Her own voice now betrayed tension.

"I already have."

Jennifer bolted upright. "I must go to him."

"No!" Peter shouted.

"Peter, I'll come back."

Peter resisted her soothing words. He wanted one emotion of his own, even if it was only jealousy.

"Meg, Daddy will put you back to bed. I'm going out for a little while, but tomorrow everything will be fine."

"It will be very different." Meg replied while busily drawing again.

"Jen--" Peter started. His thoughts and body felt pulled as if by intense gravity.

"Peter, I need you here with Meg. I'll call if I need a knight to rescue me. Don't be afraid."

Jennifer knelt and kissed Meg, and left Peter with a small, simple smile.

Peter accepted her emotional caress. Again, he watched her walk alone into the night. Once, it was to conceive Meg. Now it might be to save her, and perhaps more.

"Honey, what dragon did you set free?" Peter asked, and slowly closed the door.

Meg lifted her drawing. Peter recognized the grotesque, vest clad beast originally drawn by John Tenniel for Lewis Carroll's Through the Looking Glass.

"The Jabberwock?" Peter said with a confused, stuttered laugh.

Meg nodded affirmation. "But it will be much bigger than this."

Jennifer looked at the road ahead of her. She had always put the lives of others before her own. Even her child was born from a commitment to higher ideals. Before her birth, Meg was only an idealistic abstraction. Now she was a living person, and the daughter she loved more than anything else on Earth and any other worlds. Jennifer enjoyed her life with a child and loving husband. She wanted to preserve this paradise a little longer. However, she knew the smallest stone, when thrown by the right person, could cause waves to sweep away whole continents and all desires. Loud thunder rumbled ahead. Jennifer noticed the shadow walking beside her.

"Jennifer, I need your help." Michael stepped into three dimensions.

"Where is William? I--"

"He created my urgency," Michael interjected. "He seeks to reconstruct reality's present design."

"I don't believe it. William has always worked to preserve life, mortal and magic."

90

"For longer than civilization. And tonight he feels he still does, but life without humanity, immortal or otherwise. I would stop him, but I cannot do so alone."

"But I cannot reweave what he has done. My powers are only reactive." Jennifer felt her anxiety crest.

"That may be enough. There is a property to his spell I cannot discern. If you can find that secret within him, perhaps we can stop him."

William stood on a boulder left by glaciers over ten thousand years ago. A nearby bulldozer stood parked to tear it and the surrounding woods away. William thought the boulder made a poor altar, but a fine perch to watch his second progeny grow. Using Meg's power to amplify his spell meant it would manifest too quickly for enough of his magic siblings to arrive and thwart its birth. The dragon formed in its womb of rippling green and purple light. It still needed one, last piece to make it whole. William could stand close to this inhuman offspring. He had watched Meg grow from a promised distance that he never breached. Until tonight.

"William?" Jennifer called from behind him.

William turned and covered her with his shadow. She was still young and beautiful. Or was she? Her long, black hair was pulled tightly behind her head and streaked with gray. The wind rippled her dress across greater curves than William remembered. Once gentle eyes now focused sharply at him. Whatever beauty Jennifer held in his or other eyes no longer mattered, William thought. Soon, even her memory would cease to exist.

"Do you know what the name William means, Jennifer?" he asked. "It is a Germanic fusion for ardent protector. Ironic now, I suppose. But today William is just a collection of sounds on ears deaf to meaning. The word 'earth' means only dust."

Jennifer let him speak and patiently waited to draw out his secret. William liked to talk. He might reveal the element she needed before Jennifer said a single word of temptation. Michael watched from an insubstantial viewpoint, waiting.

"With my first language, we created words to teach survival." William continued. "Later we erected stones to honor natural forces. The priests beseeched the stones to help us, but the cold rock stayed indifferent. Weary followers finally killed the fatted priests on their own altars. I held the reddened antler-blade. I knew power to change was not locked in solid rock. I felt something more. Now, civilization subjugates the planet with indifference to nature. The future will be as barren as a stone altar. Unless I act, again."

"Humanity will learn as you did." Jennifer said. She tried to control her growing fear as William's monster grew within the light flashing beyond him. "Life has persevered before. There is reason to hope, William, not destroy."

"Hope. Another mortal idea. Like them, it is born and soon dies." William countered. "Our fate is not determined by hope, Magic, nor stone idols. Action controls destiny. Yet humanity has become the uncaring gods, or their fat priests."

"I still have hope, William. For Meg. It's not too late for her."

"It is, Jennifer." William raised his hands to the thundering clouds. "Meg's future would be a desert of despair. I will free her from that. She will always have been the jewel she is now."

"How can you condemn your child? Didn't you think of her future when she was conceived?"

"Meg was always part of my plan." William replied with grim calm. "Our union created the perfect tool to create humanity's destroyer."

Behind William the flames surged and the monster within them expanded. Fiery swirls visible within formed long, embryonic limbs.

"Meg is Earth's savior." William looked at his forming dragon. "The altar is set. The prayer is spoken. The morning sun will see an Earth reborn."

92

"No." The single word betrayed Jennifer's fear. She knew they only course left meant open confrontation with a man whose use of Magic predated written history. William carefully shrouded his plan under a cloak of time. Time was now Jennifer's enemy, as well. She saw William's monster grow. More flames curled into narrow branches of veins awaiting skin.

"You've done to your own child what you say humanity has to the Earth." Jennifer said defiantly. She gathered her strength around her on the howling wind. "I won't let you kill her!"

William smiled at Jennifer's resolve. Lightning flashed as the black storm descended before them. The clouds gave way to the swirling majesty of the galaxy. William outstretched his arms and his body flared into a brilliant comet that fell towards the spirals of the Milky Way. Jennifer's mind followed him just as soaring eagle sought its prey. She knew he wanted the awe to overwhelm her. They could go farther still. Magic touched every part of the universe at once. Jennifer stayed focused. She let him expand their battlefield within his mind until his thoughts were the size of stars, and easily revealed.

William attempted to seize her with the gravity of a massive, blue star. But Jennifer was not there to match strength against strength. Her mind soared away from the stellar trap before its pull and brilliance overwhelmed her. As William focused on laying traps to destroy her, his other thoughts would be more obvious to perceive, even if disguised as cosmic entities. Jennifer found an emotional spark deep within a coal black nebula. What shined as a hidden star was his love for Meg that he tried to bury. Just as an eagle could beat its massive wings, Jennifer fanned the spark. Its prison exploded.

The light engulfed William's conscience. Sudden grief surged through his mind. He had betrayed his own daughter. William fell from the stone against the ground and rolled onto the parking lot. He glanced across the asphalt as if looking for fragments of his shattered ego. Jennifer knelt beside him. She had won, but his monster's secret still remained concealed. Michael appeared beside her.

"I can hold him within his sorrow. Enter his mind and find--" Jennifer stopped. Her body tensed.

William stood holding his head. "A good plan, Jennifer." He strained to speak. "But, I am afraid your ally will soon leave."

"And why, old friend?" Michael asked.

"You are the spawn of Magic." William took deep breaths between each sentence. "Magic is bound to life, not humanity. When Magic acts in this world, it is to preserve life itself. Only in arrogance can humans consider themselves the sole reason." William drew a much deeper breath. "Magic grew as humanity flourished. Yet, it no longer needs the human mind to expand its awareness. Now it can do so on its own. My spell is against one species. Not all life. It doesn't threaten Magic. It will still be nurtured by life. Perhaps more so than if humanity destroys life's only cradle."

All three paused. William's monster still formed and grew. The light and charge through the air still pulsed.

"He is right, Jennifer." Michael said as if hearing a distant voice call to him. "Magic has been used by both sides of humanity, yet it has no polarity of its own. I serve its greater whole. At least for a time I knew my own will, but I cannot help you. I am sorry."

Michael faded into a shadow standing in the light, and vanished.

His departure stunned Jennifer. William pulled fiercely at the emotional bonds gripping him. Jennifer forced him back to the ground, and braced against a lamp post.

"So long as you remain, I can tear the knowledge from you!" Jennifer shouted. "Stop this, William. Or I will, and you will suffer!"

"Yes," William said staggering to the woods. "But with my loss, my actual death, there can be no going back. I am not only willing to sacrifice others, but also myself."

94

William turned and thrust his arm towards his monster, still mostly a specter of light. The beast's ghostly, serpentine neck shot downward. Jennifer screamed as the monster's head parted to reveal jaws that engulfed and snapped closed over William. A gush of red exploded into a sphere of lightning. The rippling bolts knit into flesh and scales. The last crackle of energy died at the end of dragon wings that mauled the surrounding evergreens.

Jennifer fell backward. Peter caught her from behind. She looked at him with shock, and then returned his smile. Meg walked ahead of them and stared at the beast freed from her fantasies.

"She wanted to come here," Peter explained. "I'm sorry, I couldn't stop her."

"Peter, she's only a child." Jennifer said.

"I don't think so anymore." Peter replied, and looked at the luminous beast through the trees.

The Jabberwock's large, human-like eyes glowed like aging street-lights. Yet it still seemed devoid of life's animating spark. The sound of car bumpers colliding caused Peter and Jennifer to glance to the intersection. The few late night drivers noticed the brilliant creature in the tress beyond the stores. Despite the storm winds, stopped drivers left their cars and looked at the monster in awe. All their mortal eyes focused on the thing looking back at them from above the trees.

"It's like Meg's drawing!" Peter asked. "Is it a good thing? Should we destroy it? Can we?"

"Yes." Jennifer sighed. "But there is a facet yet to be added. We need to find it."

"I was able to read parts of the book," Peter said. "It was a like a written puzzle box--"

"Oh my god!" Jennifer screamed, glancing to their sides. "Where's Meg!"

Jennifer looked at the Jabberwock. It returned her gaze with recognition as it came to life. The last facet was in place. Jennifer's heart became as cold as William's makeshift altar. It had all gone according to his plan. Jennifer screamed in defiance.

"Jen! What's happened?" Terror overtook Peter, as well.

"Meg! She's become a part of that thing. William added himself to it, to draw her in."

Peter had no words. His heart was pounding so fast and loud that it drowned out all sound.

Jennifer's strength returned. She looked at the monster with resolve. If she could not destroy it, she would certainly free her daughter. No sorcerer's spell or hideous beast would stop her. The storm ceded to an unearthly calm. Streaks of orange flared over distant mountains. Dawn had begun.

"Peter," Jennifer's voice strained with emotion, but she spared Peter his own. "Go back to the house. Bring back the books I prepared for Meg. Hurry."

The Jabberwock craned its neck and looked down at Jennifer. Something within it stirred, as if it slowly realized its purpose. Jennifer understood its design. William shaped his destroyer from a poem in an industrial age fairy tale. It wasn't a reflection of humanity or William's hatred, but of Meg and her innocence. Innocence was something all humanity shared, yet sacrificed to master the world. Jennifer knew William would consider it all poetic.

Jennifer walked to the monster through the woods. She felt Meg's mind struggling to understand what was happening. To add Meg's power to the beast, William's spell needed to bend the child's mind to willingly incorporate with it. Such strength would be overwhelming. Jennifer needed to stop that. She called to Meg. The strain of sending her voice through the maelstrom could shatter Jennifer's own mind. She focused.

As great as Meg could become, now she was a confused, frightened child. Meg heard the echo of her mother's voice through the grotesque, dragon-shaped prison. She reached out to her mother. When they linked, Jennifer imagined the days when she, Meg, and Peter would go to the local park. The memories offered peace. That peace and their bond formed a bridge. Meg followed her mother's guiding voice through the snares and decoys woven into William's spell.

Jennifer hoped that if the monster flew, it would be without Meg. It may unfold its massive wings to engulf the Earth, but with certain aspects missing that conflagration might not consume everyone. With Meg gone, only remnants of William's thoughts would guide or simply haunt the monster's mind. Without Meg's perceptions, it might not recognize children at all. They may survive. Jennifer knew such hopes were a long shot. However, as plans change and events are altered, the world can also change. That was true for all realities.

Meg stepped onto the grass of the park created by her mother. She wanted to be there, instead. She wanted out of this strange and confusing place someone tricked her to enter. She stepped toward the park. Something pulled her back. She became angry. Meg tore herself from the heart of the Jabberwock. She fell into Jennifer's arms. The Jabberwock screamed as its most powerful part was ripped away. The shockwaves of its ethereal scream shook the trees around the beast, and far beyond. The beast might heal. However, Jennifer had altered its spell.

Jennifer held Meg in the last moments of darkness. She could feel the spell of the Jabberwock unfold. What she had prepared for Meg would have to be enough. The rest she would learn. No words disturbed their last moments. As the dawn sky brightened, Jennifer faded. William's magic did its dark work. By full sunrise, she was gone. Meg fell on the ground where her mother had been to feel her last essence and warmth left in the dust. Behind her the Jabberwock lifted its grotesque wings and cast its malignant shadow. The monster was William's spell made incarnate and bonded to the Earth. It bellowed as the downward gust of its wings shook the ground. It took flight to spread the spell as night fell to each daybreak across the world, and the age of humanity ended. Yet, its spell had been altered.

Meg awoke among the trees. Her tears had mingled with the dirt to form dark streaks down her face. She walked dazed from the woods, and soon found her purpose. Other children wandered across the still, suburban landscape. Meg could feel the changes over the Earth as William's beast continued to soar. Elements of the past seemed like images in a shattered mirror. She wiped the smudges from her face. She found the family's car near the woods. Inside were the books Peter brought in his last, heroic act as her father.

The tomes were transcriptions of survival manuals and botanical guides rewritten and redrawn into leather bound manuscripts that endured reality's shifts. Meg felt her mother in the words and intricately drawn pictures. She looked again at the children gathering around her. They would need a leader.

Meg felt a strange, new turmoil within herself as both her emotions and intellect flourished. Meg realized she would wrestle with William's prejudices, having spent time as the heart of his monster. He was inside her mind, but so was Jennifer. It would be easy to bend the children to her will, or destroy them. It would be harder to help them so they all survived in the new dawn her mother created.

Meg felt a presence, and turned. A boy dressed in black with saffron hair stood in the shadow of the woods.

"Go away," Meg said. She didn't fully understand her instinctive rejection, other than a feeling he shared responsibility in the loss of her mother.

The boy vanished. His smiled faded more slowly than the rest of him. Meg knew she would see him again. By then she hoped to find a path between the shifting images of the old world and the new reality shinning through. The next few hours would be harsh. The next week would be even worse. Winter was coming. She stared at the bewildered children. They were all too human. And so was she. They would need to find warmth together. Meg hoped soon, before the darkness fell again. She would help them all, starting now.

Meg awoke. She was rising. She was within her mother's arms as she stood. Jennifer, spoke to her. The words were soothing. It was dawn, but they weren't at home. Her father guided them into the car, and they drove away from the stores and small forest. She recalled what had happened in the night. She had been in the heart of a monster, and the monster held a foot on many worlds. She had experienced the first hours after dawn in several realities. This was the one she wanted. Here, there was no monster, anymore. This was home.

Her mother kissed her head. Her father looked back at them and smiled. Meg's face crinkled into an expression of joy. She chose this as her final reality. And so it would be. There were still many Halloweens to come. Meg would enjoy as many as she could along with her family, and perhaps an odd friend or two that stepped out of shadows.

HEAVEN FOR PENNIES

Planet Earth rolled slowly below the long traveled ship. The silver cylinder reflected the Sun's naked rays as it descended towards a cloud bank high in the atmosphere. The ship had transversed a great distance by slipping the effects of spacetime and avoiding catastrophic collisions through this solar system and others. Maintaining the straight line to the planet's surface would only appear simple. It required accounting for a vast number of orbital satellites and space debris. The pilots didn't want to annoy the local inhabitants with careless impacts. Even the structure of the ship was designed to promote favor. The cylinder was the most innocuous and accepted shape across the spectra of galactic intelligent. The pilots had vast experience in finding approval, and imagined Earth would be no different. The small, blue world harbored countless lifeforms, and a sentient species with an ever-expanding population. It was this species that enticed the great, silver ship to Earth. The alien translation for humanity was: new customers.

"Damn!" Phil Jaccobs barked. He strained to maneuver his large, new, and scrape-free pick-up truck through the congested and bustling parking lot of the All-America Mega Mall. He was aiming for an open spot, only to see his prized destination filled by a small, nimble hybrid car. Phil slammed his palm against his truck's steering wheel. He shook his hand from the pain, and looked to see if he'd marked the leather cover. He then glanced to see if his buddy Tate Lincomb noticed his childish fury.

Tate was used to Phil's anger. He was always annoyed at something. Usually it was Tate. But he'd known Phil for so long that Phil's voice and curt comments were almost just background noise. That, and Phil did buy them beer. Tate liked beer. He also liked going to the mall. There was always something to see. Today, his surprise went far beyond Phil's new truck.

It was sunny. Tate liked looking out. Sunny weather meant sparse clothing. Not that Tate liked revealing his lack of fitness, but he enjoyed fitness in the women walking from their cars. Two such women crossed in front of Phil's truck.

"How did they find a spot?" Phil barked. "Man, why aren't you looking for a spot?"

"'Cause I was looking at them." Tate answered.

"Well, look for a place to park!"

After a second of Tate's silence, Phil glanced over at him. Tate stared far above the asphalt. Tate rolled down the passenger-door widow and stuck his head outside.

"You see one?" Phil barked.

"I see something." Tate said. "It's big. Real big."

"If you're talking about some gal--!"

"Nope." Tate rarely cut off Phil because he seldom listened to what he said. This time Tate wanted Phil to just listen.

"Phil, look up! Just look up!"

"Why? I can't park on the roof, you nut!"

"I think this is real."

"This is real annoying!" Phil squeaked. "Hell, you're annoying."

"Yeah." Tate never glanced away from the sky. "Just stop the truck. I think it's aliens."

"Tate, man! You're an alien."

"Then my family just docked over the mall." Tate said and opened the door while the truck slowly moved forward. "Look, see ya."

Tate hopped out of the truck and began walking toward the mall, always looking skyward.

"Hey!" Phil hit the brakes. He watched Tate enter a crowd looking up and heading for the mall. Only a few people stood still, but also stared skyward. Fewer people rushed back to their cars as if to flee. Most of them carried too many shopping bags in front of their faces to even see straight ahead.

Phil eyed a passing sedan with side mirrors edging dangerously close to his truck's still-perfect paint job.

A scrape on his new truck was just one of several increasing concerns that caused Phil's stomach and attitude to churn. The down payment for the truck he truly couldn't afford and all the other bills coming due meant all the cash he had was a few twenty dollar bills in his wallet. His credit was maxed out. Today he hoped Tate would pay for lunch and the beer. At least just the beer. He was glad he didn't have a family or anyone depending on him. Anyone other than Tate. But he usually just wanted a ride. Driving Tate's couch was Phil's only option if he lost his job. Phil hated that. A woman carrying a small dog a few cars over waved to Phil and jabbed her finger to the sky above the mall. Even her dog was starring skyward. Phil finally looked up.

The great, silver cylinder slowly finished the last length of its journey exactly centered over the mall. Its only hint of energy came from flashes as if rainbows were caught from the sky along invisible seems spiraling down the sides. The bands of color flared into brilliant sparks. The flashes stopped as the ship halted and hovered silently over the mall's highest skylight.

Phil parked his new truck in the traffic lane. He jumped out of the cab and hustled to catch up to Tate. A throng gawking at the floating ship slowed his progress. Phil found the slow moving people aggravating.

The ship seemed impossibly still. Soon, its placid occupants appeared. However, there was no grand exit. No one saw them leave. No announcement boomed to the crowd from an otherworldly voice. Those who stayed outside to watch the ship were disappointed. Some shoppers inside began to hear about a commotion out in the parking lot. Then a murmur grew as a small number of people noticed the few long-traveled aliens walking among them. The small, prism-skinned, and ovate extraterrestrials with turquoise eyes moved through the crowds just as experienced shoppers with a memorized floor plan. Yet, most shoppers were so accustomed to sophisticated visual promotions and sensory assaults, that the aliens hardly warranted attention. Many people kept wagging battles for overpriced 'sale' merchandise and complaining about the quality of mass-produced food served on paper and plastic. It was only when mall security interrupted the alien's unscheduled presentation that most exhausted, newly insolvent people took note.

Phil Jaccobs took note. He fingered the twenties inside his wallet. Phil wanted the strangely accented sales-pitch to continue. Those looking at phone and tablet screens saw more of it simultaneously broadcast and translated across planet Earth. The aliens and their ads offered all humanity freedom from toil, and an everlasting life of permanent bliss. And all for the affordable price of forty nine ninety-five, US.

The aliens remained composed when manhandle by the guards. But vivid concern knit their kaleidoscopic faces when considered nothing more than a prank, even after their radiant sphere appeared. It glowed as if lit by spectral fires. After the mall's management received quadruple the demonstration fee in pure gold, the strange, little pitch-men continued. To recapture consumer interest, they offered their service to a limited number, free of charge.

Louise Guilfoyle had participated in mall demos before, unconsciously trying to compensate for failing junior high drama class decades earlier. Few among the gathered voiced concern after the glowing orb descended over her, and her body fell to the stage. A murmur echoed when the number of bodies rose to six. An off duty paramedic examined the human pile while audience members were asked to communicate with the fallen. The aliens explained the participants were now happy inhabitants of the glowing sphere. Horror and outrage overtook the paramedic after finding just gleeful smiles on frigid remains. He rushed screaming at the aliens. All sensation vanished behind a curtain of black. When it lifted, the aliens and their glowing ball were gone. Left behind were seven bodies of once skeptical volunteers, and one impromptu participant.

Phil Jaccobs was left holding out his cash to an empty stage. As the crowd dispersed, he saw the shocked look on Tate's face several paces away. Phil only shrugged and pocked his money. He withdrew his new truck's keys and tossed them over to Tate. He stayed staring up at the empty stage. He was certain the aliens would return, and certain he'd never have to make another payment on anything, ever again.

There were more problems establishing a market on Earth than the aliens anticipated. Military firepower assaulted their alien ship. They kindly apologized for weathering the attack without damage, and reiterated that this was simply an unfortunate misunderstanding. They said they were here to sell a service, not savage a planet. While the United Nations met in anxious solidarity to deal with the extraterrestrial menace, the aliens themselves calmly presented their case to the global public. Their ads ran on satellite television. Interactive spam and colorful ads littered the internet. Celebrity talk shows and video magazines vied for the appearance of the prismatic and gracious guests. Shortly, the aliens reached an agreement with Earth's leaders. Governments needed to act with unity and record speed or get left out of the alien experience now intimate to their citizens. The aliens invited relatives of the 'mall fallen' to visit with their now non-corporeal loved ones.

The aliens explained their non-paying customers were still very much in existence. Death, as understood by humans, was an outdated concept. The complete electro-chemical structure of a person's memory and personality was transferred inside the glowing container. The sphere would then be their home for the rest of time. To use a human analogy, their soul ascended into the eternal energy of the sphere. The relatives confirmed that their loved ones were indeed inside the sphere, and experienced the promised peace and happiness. Many said they had paid the aliens (who were given an account by a speculating Liechtenstein bank) so they could join the eternal

104

bliss. With peace and licensing agreements reached, the modest feeling of urgency that griped the planet at last relaxed. The international news services quickly switched to coverage of the next world crisis, which had patiently waited for their cameras.

Phil Jaccobs' patience was rewarded. The aliens returned to the mall, this time inside a new storefront. Phil had spent all his cash on mall food. He got a loan of fifty bucks from Tate Lincomb. Tate still liked the mall if not the new alien shop inside it. He was still driving Phil's truck, so he thought the fifty was only fair. He owed Phil a lot more for gas, anyway. Phil was not alone. The number of interested customers grew exponentially.

An actual afterlife was now attainable, and, perhaps, easier to afford than traditional and uncertain predecessors. World society whirled from the possibility. Death was no longer the dark harbinger at life's end. Now, only taxes were inevitable. However, anyone could cheat them for a reasonable price. As the cost was the same for both poor and affluent, many wealthy people bought the service under assumed names.

"But how can you promise eternal peace so cheaply?" was asked of the aliens at every media event they organized or attended. Their answer was very similar to one grafted on the collective unconscious of all shopping network viewers: "We can provide our service at this amazing discount because of our sales volume on other worlds."

"But how can your customers be sure your claims are true?"

"It's a no-risk venture," the aliens would calmly affirm. "If you're not satisfied with the total bliss provided, we will re-corporeate your consciousness, and you'll receive a full refund. We guarantee it!"

A convincing display of unsolicited testimonials by other types of aliens increased consumer confidence. Scientists pointed out the more astonishing fact that plenty of alien species existed to offer testimonials. However, it was as if human culture had been preparing for a time when the reality of multiple aliens with multiple eyes, multiple arms, and even multiple sexes was normal. Sociologists wondered if such acceptance would exist after this was eventually true in supermarkets and neighborhood daycares.

There were still more concerns among governments, banks, Wall Street, and those deft at larceny. A substantial issue was integrating Earth's economy with others across the galaxy. The concept of 'buy local' now meant more than at the farmer's market. Protectionism became a common policy. Most investors decided that they would rather buy an alien service on Earth rather than trust their hedge funds or retirement to complex financial formulas that included gravitational interaction, and where inflation meant spatial expansion caused by dark energy. The motto 'Buy alien, Invest Terran' became popular. The aliens of course, invested in both, free of fear and seeing no end in a human market because of Homo sapiens' great desire to breed beyond ecological barriers. In fact, as well as providing a means of afterlife, they aided in creating future life by investing in Earth's already robust pornographic industry.

Yet, there were detractors on the quickly altering Earth. Some would die considering the aliens and/or their claims a fantastic hoax, generated by computers. Despite these lost customers, and the trite but expected charges of satanic evil, business became brisk. The most ardent and unique denouncement came not from religious, nor consumer-watch groups, but from the unfortunate nuclear annihilation of St. Petersburg, Florida by 'true death' extremists. The mostly geriatric terrorists claimed that only a complete end of existence could bring eternal peace. In a display of good will, the aliens erected a memorial monument. However, their Public Relations firm quickly re-commissioned the plaque after discovering the alien's wording was mostly sympathetic to the loss of prime real estate for centuries. Despite such gestures and advertising, word of mouth remained the most powerful form of promotion. People related the stories of those close to them who made one last leap of faith.

Faith meant little to some. Dale Harding knew only the life of a reporter. He had seen history be committed directly before his eyes. Now he struggled to record his experiences after a brief communion with the sphere. The sensation of total peace was difficult to describe for a man so jaded and emotionally callused. His acidic stomach began to roil anew. Throughout his life he thought all the pain was worth it to expose the truth. Now, he wondered.

"Caught you looking." The husky voice of Marnie Hask broke Dale's reverie.

Dale was surprised that Marnie spoke to him, first. Yet, there was no one else across the wide expanse of desks and cubicle's this late. Marnie's comment accused Dale of a personal infraction, although Dale stared only at his computer's keyboard. Dale and Marnie once had a romantic tryst. It was one night that spurred a decade of sharp looks if Dale's gaze ever drifted towards her desk. Dale never knew if it was an inside joke or punishment.

"I need to find an angle." Dale said blankly. He turned his chair and dared to look straight at Marnie's blue eyes flaring out from under artificial blonde bangs.

"I got mine." Marnie said. "We're doomed."

Dale's face flashed to wide-eyed surprise. The shock came as Marnie pulled out a pack of cigarettes from her desk and lit one inside the office. Company policy banned the act years before it became illegal.

"They can fire, me." Marnie blew smoke at Dale. She turned and waved to a ceiling camera.

They both knew the newspaper had cut the cameras and security to save money. Dale hoped that the fire sprinklers still worked, but would only flip on after he left the floor.

"You think this is some clever attack?" Dale asked.

"No. This is no invasion." Marnie drew a long drag. "But the little turquoise-eyed freaks will end up running the place."

"Huh," was Dale's considered reply. But he saw Marnie's point. Almost all humanity would pay out the small fee for the sense of utter and complete freedom. Dale recalled his own touch with the sphere. He was almost in tears when the sensation was gone.

"Yep." Dale nodded. "Not a lot of checks and balances on it. Yet."

"Just think," Marnie said. "The dream of a winning lotto ticket? Forget it. Now it's the dream of a bus ride to a mall or store, and an upload into an overgrown Christmas tree ornament."

"Go wild. Hire a taxi."

"No kidding." Marnie exhaled more smoke. "The fare is more than the fee for eternity."

"Why are they doing it?" Dale was curious if Marnie could float him new insight through her personal smog bank.

"Because they can. And they like a buck."

"They got a lot more bucks, now." Dale waved away the smoky curtain between them. "I hear there's a call for a universal dollar, backed by the aliens to make their accounting easier."

"See, I told you they'll run the show." Marnie nodded. She looked for a makeshift ash tray, but not even a trash can was close by. She flicked the ashes from her cigarette behind her.

"You think that's a good thing?" Dale asked, and stood.

"It can't get much worse." Marnie shrugged. "There's no more ice in the arctic."

"Someone should offer eternal bliss to polar bears."

"They can't afford it."

"Maybe the Canadian government will chip in for them." Dale smiled.

"No lobbyists." Marnie took another drag.

108

"What about the Ever Green Earth Society?"

"They're just gonna sit back and watch Earth green up again with less people." Marnie flicked more ash behind her.

"What do you think the alien planet is like? Do they have arctic ice?"

"They got a lot of green. They can buy ice."

"You got an extra one?" Dale asked while eying Marnie's pack.

"No. I gave up smoking. Company policy." Marnie gently wiggled her cigarette in her fingers.

Dale frowned. Marnie smiled.

"When my Dad was real young, he worked where everybody puffed." Dale said.

"Hopefully they did a lot more of what comes first, at home." Marnie said.

"Lighting up?"

"No, you delete! The sex." Marnie's brown eyebrows shot up under her blonde bangs.

"I'm an only child." Dale sighed, and then coughed.

"You got kids?" Marnie asked.

Dale thought that was an odd question from a woman he once had sex with. He thought his return question was even stranger.

"No. You?"

"Nope." Marnie pulled a thick stack of clean paper from the printer's tray. She crushed her cigarette into it. "Never wanted them."

"Well, with enough people like us, there won't be any humans running around anymore." Dale sighed, and then coughed.

"Then it's down to polar bears."

"Actually, they're now extinct." Dale said.

"Too bad." Marnie shrugged. "So I guess the aliens will have to manage the herd. If they want future customers."

"Would you do it?" Dale cocked an eyebrow.

"You, again?"

"No!" Dale was proud of his honest disgust. "I mean the sphere."

"Nope." Marnie said.

"Why?"

"It's like an overdose." Marnie shoved the wad of paper under her desk. "One last whiff and it's over."

"But you don't die."

"If I'm not wearing this," Marnie pulled the skin on the back her hand. "Then, I ain't alive."

"You are going to die, one day."

"Well, you first, Dale. Here. Get started." Marie pushed the pack of cigarettes towards Dale.

"Yeah." Dale rubbed his aching stomach. He left Marnie's pack untouched. He walked to the elevator lobby without a backward glance. Eight hours later, he missed his first deadline. An hour after that, he made his last transaction for forty-nine ninety-five.

Like Dale Harding from his ulcers, deliverance was at hand for the common worker. Employers not motivated to end it all still required a work force. Wages plummeted as workers left jobs and lived off savings, waiting for the chance to purchase bliss with the one fifty dollar bill held tighter than any family heirloom. The aliens could keep the change. Governments with rapidly decreasing tax bases quickly enacted legislation to legalize the fall of pay and more Draconian policies. One the other side of society, the aliens, who never did offer their names, became a fixture in Earth's quickly changing social hierarchy. Their presence enriched official functions, trade shows, and even ecclesiastical conventions. They found new customers at all events. The unexpected endorsement and subsequent disappearance of Pope Urban X ensured sales and a loyal customer base.

The aliens always claimed that expanding the market of eternal life was their only motivation to leave their self-described homeworld paradise. They said their own sphere made that happy condition possible. The aliens continued earthly residence created its own host of motivations. They paid all business and occupation taxes; licensing; patent fees; and bribes in cash. Tourism increased in the state where their ship arrived. Ultimately, the silver gleam from the cylinder lit the way for the state's Governor to become President. Heaven became a reality not just for their customers, but for the social and political entrepreneur with the right connections.

As a result of the cultural and economic upheavals—and the real prospect of humanity disappearing altogether—a 'Code of Ascension' was written with full alien support. Mandatory procreation replaced all population controls. Consumers needed to reach a minimum age of thirty before ascension. However, visiting your ascended loved ones via trans-corporeal up-links meant the Earth bound could share in the peace and love at regimented intervals while awaiting their ascension. Soon after, illegal Soul Dens flourished in the temporal underworld. They outpaced powerful new narcotics as the favored way to 'get high.'

Change seemed exponential, to those who bothered to notice. The only constant in the human equation was the image of the glowing sphere. The artificial immortality became a permanent part of life. Old concepts and their physical expressions were razed and paved over. Unfortunately, the number of catastrophic injuries rose dramatically. All of which seemed to carefully avoid causing brain damage. The special early release for the disabled was revoked. Accidents soon ebbed. However, an architectural result of the alien's service was the proliferation of small-scaled sky scrapers, as more and more people wished to have the dangerous job of hanging I-beams at little or no pay, so long as adequate brain protection equipment was provided.

Closer to the ground, there was no longer an emotional need for cemeteries as the desire to preserve the body died itself. Below the surface, new communities of detritus eaters flourished at the oceans' bottom. Religions also mutated to incorporate the tangible afterlife provided by the aliens. Some

111

claimed it was the paradise promised all along, and once you crossed over you could communicate with the dead from ages past. The aliens neither confirmed nor denied this postulation, having created the concept of the customer always being right millennia before humanity discovered barter.

Eventually, there was no longer a feeling of dread with increasing age. Instead, joy rose with advancing years, however few their number. In the courts, the ultimate punishment was no longer execution, but banning entrance to the sphere. Voluminous law suits filed by the International Civil Liberties Union caused the bans to be overturned. The alien created afterlife became a fundamental human right. Judicial sanction came more easily after the proprietors' assurances that no violence could occur, nor was such an act possible, once a person ascended. Political candidates continued to find employment by claiming a vote for them would be a vote for the continued access to eternal peace for all who could afford it.

In time came an end to war, now considered too dangerous to precious gray matter. Advances in the leisurely pursuit of science brought an end to suffering. Resources increased for all with the spherical population control in place. The greatest number of languid, leisure pursuits ever known eased physical existence. Yet, people still needed to earn payment for the procedure. The cost of which had progressively risen due to decreased sales volume, and, of course, increasing operating costs.

An anticipated side-effect of the increased cost was the proliferation of illegal Soul Dens. They continually improved in technology and camouflage. Just as in the age of illicit drugs, some found employment in the endless task of their eradication. Alderson was a typical example of humanity for his era. He was beautiful to any aesthetic measure, and possessed physical capabilities rivaling any Homeric hero. However, he rarely needed them as a transcendental police officer. His partner in maintaining proper access to the sphere's halcyon daze was one of the aliens themselves. It had volunteered for the menial task of patrolling psyche-space out of a peculiar affection for the Terran natives. Their office was the interior of a large, luminous globe with access to all the information coursing across Earth and beyond. Two chairs floated in the spherical room's center. Both seats were typically facing the same direction, usually oriented to the equator.

Alderson watched the real-time image of the Earth roll slowly across the curved walls. He was one year away from leaving his job and physical existence to join the other sphere. This looming event had spurred questions in an otherwise certain mind.

"If attainment of spherical peace is mortal humanity's destiny, then why not provide it for all at once?" He asked his partner in the high, thesaurial manner currently passing for colloquial English.

"The logistical constraints make that impossible." The alien answered after a pause. He—that was Alderson's assumption—liked to indulge the latest human-created fad of reading information printed on paper. Although, readers needed to keep buying new pages to keep pace with upgrades. He found Alderson's query more interesting. His human partner wasn't typically philosophical.

"What prevented all the members of your species from eventually entering its own sphere?" Alderson furthered.

"Like humanity's leaders, ours had the foresight to forestall a complete biological dissolution. Besides, someone had to bring it to other worlds." The alien offered. It still spoke in the twenty-first century dialect it mastered long ago.

"That is, at best, an oblique answer." Alderson was unsatisfied.

"I believe I can answer your questions with another from Earth's past," the alien replied with growing amusement. "Which came first, the chicken or the egg?"

"That is ridiculous," Alderson said with disgust. "How can that provide elucidation?"

"Perspective," the alien chirped. "When we did research to see if this planet was a suitable market, this was one argument we scrutinized to understand the human psyche. At first it perplexed us. Time spent on the argument, I mean."

"But that question is inherently ludicrous," Alderson said. "If chickens descended from sexually dimorphic creatures, then the ova must precede any such species, or its constituent individuals."

"Certainly true," the alien replied. "But such a conclusion can only come from transcending the parameters of the argument to understand the greater whole. Ultimately, we came to the conclusion that if a race spent so much time with an argument of such limited scope, they would be perfect candidates for our services. However, it also can provide answers to your questions."

Alderson prompted the alien's conclusion with a look of disbelief.

"Something must first create the situation—in a purely linear sense. Temporal distortions notwithstanding. Thus, full consideration must include the agency of creation. Only then can clear insight be found." Turquoise eyes looked up at Alderson.

Mentally, Alderson felt like a spider having caught an invisible fly in its web. Something important now tore at the geometry of his world. He sensed the alien had revealed more about themselves, and the merits of their service, than the scope of the discussion seemed to encompass. He thought that might be the whole point.

"So then there is something other than biological dissolution that prevents your species from completely entering the sphere." Alderson watched the alien's response.

It remained silent, as if not wanting to move and thus guide the spider towards its goal. But Alderson was a persistent predator, and plucked the web's strands to jostle his prey.

"So your species have become interplanetary chickens, depositing your precious eggs where agreeable." Alderson said.

"An unfortunate advancement of the model. But, in essence, yes. However, we are more like farmers than chickens." The alien replied with a shade of pride showing through the otherwise placid mien.

"Ah," Alderson said, sensing he was closer to his target. "You are instead harvesters, rather than depositors."

"Yes," the alien responded in a favorable tone.

"And so, to harvest you need to manage your flock. And your eggs." Alderson fell silent. He had thought he was about to strike his prey. Instead, he felt as if struck by venom. He realized humanity's place on this imaginary farm. His other mental image was also disappointing. The circular pattern of the web had led back to him. Humanity had become a managed resource.

"Your work is not without merit." The alien said, seeking to press its own advantage now that Alderson's realization seemed to hit him with a collective case of buyer's remorse for his entire species. "The laws we serve were created to provide direction. Without some boundaries there would be chaos."

The alien's voice expressed comradeship and reassurance. It attempted to realign Alderson's position in its favor like a salesman at the return desk.

"Yet, we ensure the status quo," Alderson replied, now regaining his focus. "Like the farmer ensuring his cows find green pastures."

The alien expressed his dissatisfaction of Alderson's further farm reference with an all too human sigh.

"Don't make it sound so ulterior, Alderson." It replied, blending amity with disclaimer. "Your species enjoyed many myths about everlasting peace before we arrived. We only brought that to reality. Now, many live vicariously through the soul dens to reaffirm their own desire for immortality. No herd has been so willing to graze as your own."

"Yet, without this pasture you provide, humanity had never been so close to, well, chaos, however peaceful its genesis." Alderson observed the images from the now completely verdant expanse of the northern Africa. "Once, human science created methodologies to unveil the workings of Earth and the cosmos. Our art and literature provided ways to understand them, and ourselves."

Alderson's eyes saw the projection of Earth, but his mind displayed the known arc of human history from cave to sphere.

"Some humans still do these things." The alien said. "I see a synthesis of them in mathematics. It is a method used to quantify what may seem chaotic. Yet, it must follow a system of rules to provide consistency within itself. Even so, you can enjoy mathematics purely in the abstract. As such, it's a high-order art form. It's one that can also provide greater understanding. Look at how your own consistent actions here maintain order."

"But your own species' motivations are for exploitation, rather than order, or eternal peace. Thus you need formulas, and numbers like me for it to function." Alderson asserted.

"We never claimed to be missionaries, Alderson." The alien replied. It now felt free to speak frankly.

"Just profiteers," Alderson added.

The alien remained silent.

"Chickens and spiders." Alderson mused.

The alien raised his facial equivalent of an eyebrow that caused a small rainbow to flare above turquoise.

"Cows and formulas." Alderson added.

"What do you mean?" The alien sensed it would need another human partner before their shift ended.

"I shall no longer be a number, or tend the farm." Alderson said with regret, but also a growing sense of liberty. "My employment in this office is now terminated."

"Oh, so? What will you do, then?" The alien asked with pride in Alderson's decision that it would be sure to mask from its fellow aliens.

116

"I think I shall become a mathematician," Alderson offered. "They are good at plotting trajectories off of well-maintained pastures."

"One cannot account for every variable, I guess." The alien said as it watched Alderson launch himself from his chair for the exit portal. The now empty chair began to rotate out of sync with the alien's seat.

In the Eden-like Earth's future, the seeds of Alderson's realization would fully blossom. When needing a spike of liquid assets to fend off a buy-out attempt of their Antarctic resort for extraterrestrials, the aliens decided to sell the technology of their ship's drive. A buyer's group of retrograde thinkers called 'Aldies' purchased the technology. They set out in epic fashion across the galaxy. Others followed. They colonized and conquered new worlds. Occasionally some would conquer each other in what Earth now considered mildly embarrassing interstellar wars. Many others sought and found their destinies in exploration and analysis. The realms of the universe proved more fantastic than the seekers' dreams. Beyond Earth, human knowledge grew to a size greater than the galaxy's borders.

Generations later, one descendant returned to her ancestor's mother world. Olympic in size and bearing, she bore a name consisting of a mathematical function applied to musical notes at frequencies above twenty thousand vibrations per second. She intended to add Earth to her empire, or destroy it. A group of the placid aliens greeted her with gifts and proper vocalization. They instead interested her in the concept of franchise marketing. Intrigued and placated, she purchased the marketing rights to the seemingly immortal alien's service. The aliens themselves now sought new challenges of their own, and were eager to exploit their new found markets on other worlds in selling baked goods and macramé art.

When asked why they never used their own service, one of the ship's alien replied: "Then who would bring the doughnut to Andromeda?"

"That would be a long journey," someone commented.

"Time is something we have sort of a monopoly on," another alien cryptically remarked. Then their silver ship vanished. Their holding companies left the only trace of their former presence and great impact on planet Earth.

Shortly thereafter, the sphere's new owner made an attempt to export her wares to a moderately advanced planet. Not wanting to frighten the populace, the franchise ship entered orbit and lowered its shields in a display of openness and trust. Almost instantly, an orbiting atomic weapons satellite annihilated it. The weapon served a planetary power where an orthodox talk-show host had fanned the populace into a frenzy of isolationism and paranoia. Other markets proved more difficult. Force of arms found occasional employment. However, the sale of immortality found many more buyers, especially at such an affordable price.

True to the aliens word the glowing sphere lasted the rest of time. It survived the death of Sol, and all galactic calamities. Though outside a universe rippled and flowed with change, inside there was nothing but peace. When the forces that bound the cosmos grew old and threatened to give rise to its fiery rebirth, the distant progeny of Alderson's followers encountered the Terran sphere. Inside still dwelled those who unimaginably long ago paid for release from toil and mortality for constant, never ending, terminal joy. For a moment the shimmering intellects seemed to recognize a kinship with those inside the doomed container. And then they were gone. They left the siblings of their ancestors in blissful ignorance of their certain doom to complete their own evolution into the consciousness that would shape the next creation. It would be an awesome task, and would mean their eventual self-sacrifice. Yet, what they would leave behind would be a monument greater than their own existence.

As the newly reborn fires of creation sundered the sphere's wall, a thought suddenly became clear inside the glittering haze that composed the consciousness of Louise

Guilfoyle. Life's essence flowed along the edge of an emotion indistinguishable between fear and exhilaration. It was identical to the sensation experienced by humanity's ancestors the first time they ventured from the sheltering trees into the savanna and felt a sudden urge to run into the grass. However, for Louise and all with her it was too late. For most, multiple billions of years of existence vanished without as much as a memory of yesterday. Next to Louise, the consciousness of Phil Jaccobs had been parked for a very long time. He felt the constant bliss that enwrapped him abruptly vanish. His first concern in countless millennia was whether the bank ever took his truck from Tate Lincomb, and then if it was too late for a refund.

The first second of the new universe brought new possibilities, channeled into probability, and finally certainty by vast intellects. Those minds were ultimately descended from the species that once included Louise and Phil. Their paths diverged in the shadow of the sphere. At that point, some looked to the challenge of new savannas and continued experience. The struggle to persevere led to intelligence with the power to face, and now shape, reality. That ability cost a little more than forty-nine ninety-five, yet proved a very good investment in time.

AFTER THE FIRE

The howl of the wind above overwhelmed the airlock's sharp hiss. Khofi walked up the hidden steps and into the storm. His walking stick pierced the new layer of desert. Sunlight and mirages usually defined the world outside. Now, swift ochre curtains threatened Khofi's bearings and beat against his hood. The dust laden wind nearly pushed the old man from his path, but Khofi walked on. His reason to brave the outside came into view, untouched by the storm. A towering human figure stood within a faint blue glow as his will kept the winds at bay.

Khofi gripped the sides of his hood and paused a moment to accustom himself to the fiery eyes of Tyr. He had arrived outside Khofi's village, proclaimed his benevolence, and vowed to protect its people. Tyr's kind had risen from humanity, and recreated the known worlds in their image. They laid out an empire of earthly delights for themselves and mortals. Then, because it had been foretold, they made war and turned it all into dust. Their creation burned in a purge of celestial fire. Eventually, so did the gods. All but one. Now he waited for Khofi through the squall of dust.

Khofi pressed forward. He was a child at the endtime, Ragnarok. He grew into a survivor, and taught others his skills. Now he was an old man. His brown skin had wrinkled. His strong limbs had weakened. Tyr was as striking and powerful as when he was God of War. Had he wanted to destroy Khofi's village and its legacy of hard work and perseverance, he could do so at any time. Khofi hoped Tyr's promise of benevolence meant he was open to reason, perhaps now, if not before the war. However old Khofi had become, the village was still his to protect. He stopped and stood before Tyr to do just that.

"Greetings, old mortal." Tyr's voice was clear and resonant. It vibrated across Khofi's bony frame as if his body was one large ear. "I have waited for you. I shall stay here for you, and the village dug deep into the earth. It is well hidden, but I see it and the lives within. They all shall know the protection of Tyr."

"I see." Khofi swallowed. His agon with godhood had begun. He straightened his shoulders and raised his voice against the wind. "It is not boldness that guides my words, Tyr. It is time. I have little of it left. If I stay in the storm or beneath the sun too long, either can destroy me as surely as an angry god. So, I shall be direct. It is not in disrespect of you, or your power."

"Speak freely, little man. No harm shall come to you as long as you stand beside Tyr."

Khofi heard a crackle and shuddered as energy enveloped him. It became cool. The wind and dust no longer assailed him. The storm visible beyond Tyr was now cast in a faint shimmer of azure.

"Though you have protected my body, Tyr, I hope my mind is still my own to control."

"It is. I am not here to rule you. As you are a lasting vestige of humanity, I am here to protect you all. And, when necessary, to guide you."

"It is that guidance I fear the most, Tyr."

"Explain yourself."

Khofi heard the timbre of Tyr's voice change. Still, he did not sound angry. Khofi noticed another sound coming from the distance, perhaps magnified by Tyr's aegis. It was more a rhythmic vibration through the ground. It was unnatural, and it grew stronger. In Khofi's memory, only marching soldiers made a similar sound. Khofi's curiosity would have to wait. Tyr's eyes demanded an answer.

"You and your kind protected and guided humanity before, Tyr. There were many people then, civilizations, not a single village. How much more of your guidance can we survive?"

Tyr raised his metallic right hand. Khofi stood fast. The only thing that fell was the wind. The storm subsided by either Tyr's will or its natural passing. Unfiltered sunlight lit the ochre landscape. Khofi could see the edge of the plateau that concealed his village. Below them, the desert spread to the blue horizon. The rhythmic sound was now louder. Khofi could see it did not worry Tyr, who was massive, glimmering, and power incarnate. Khofi studied his gauntlet as it came to rest against the god's side. Armor fused to the surviving stump replaced Tyr's limb long ago. Legend said Tyr lost the limb through the treachery of his fellow gods. And still he stood with them at the endtime. Khofi suspected pride favored the metal arm over growing new flesh. He set aside questions about vanity and loyalty among gods. Tyr's ability to honor the wishes of Khofi's people was vital. The old man knew it would not be what the god desired.

"What you say is true, little man." Tyr looked out across the desert as if seeing another world. "Yet, I do not come here to change history or alter time. I come to help your future. I am the last of the gods. I have chosen your village to protect and foster. It is a flourishing garden within the barren Earth."

"Many have worked to make it so. Our success is measured in mortal lives, not acts of gods. It will persist that way. That is why, Tyr, powerful though you are, we have no need of you. And so I want you to leave."

Khofi's breaths were shallow as he waited the long seconds for Tyr's answer.

"You are brave, mortal. Yet, you are old. I am eternal. What of your people once you have become dust yourself?"

"It will be as it is now. The people will survive. They will adapt. All I know has been taught to the young and recorded, lest they forget. Others more creative than I will lead. I am meaningless."

"But you are the only one facing a god."

Khofi thought that perhaps he saw Tyr's stern face bend slightly into a smile.

"True, Tyr. As I said, I am meaningless. The village is not."

122

"I like you, old man. Tell me your name."

"I am Khofi."

"Khofi, know that the memory of Tyr shall preserve you."

"Thank you. Now, please go."

Tyr was again silent for a long moment. The marching sound was now louder. Khofi wondered if it a measure of Tyr's mood, yet it rose up from the desert below.

Tyr lowered his head to stare directly at Khofi. "Can you see the future in all the years you have lived? Do you not realize what I can do for your people, especially in time of disaster?"

Khofi swallowed. "There were disasters before the gods. There will likely be one in this new age. If we can, humanity will survive. We survived you and your terrible war. We survived your pantheon's doom. We will continue into the future by our wits." Khofi looked away from Tyr's brilliant eyes and toward the horizon. He gestured with his stick and felt an itch. Beneath his cloak he retrieved a stowaway, most likely from the edges of the village. He cupped the red ant in his hand and held it to Tyr. "If ants can survive on instinct, surely humanity can think of a way to live on."

"Is life enough, Khofi? What of prosperity? I can assure that you thrive, and one day, move beyond tunnels in rock and earth. In time, humanity may again know a golden age."

"Humanity knew such an age, and we saw it burn." As Khofi spoke, his small stowaway ran within and over his cupped hands. "Now we rebuild, and by our own designs. Yet, our village is more than a human world. Ants harvest some of the moisture and fungus we cultivate. In doing so, they spread the spores and help it grow. We and the other species form an ecology of survivors. And yet the ants do not see us as gods."

Tyr extended his right hand and let the ant crawl from Khofi's frail hands onto his massive, golden fingertips. Tyr's heavy gaze seemed to weigh down the scrambling insect. It stopped its darting path.

"They do not see what they cannot comprehend, little Khofi. And what of your own present? Do you not see what I can do for you now?"

Tyr pointed with his left hand to the source of the rhythmic sound beyond the edge of the plateau. Khofi cautiously crept forward and looked down. Another unforeseen challenge threatened from the desert floor. It was an army, and closer than Khofi imagined. They had kept marching through the storm. Only peering directly over the edge could Khofi see them far below at the rocky base of the plateau. Their weapons glinted in the stark sunlight.

"An army in a desert." Khofi wondered aloud. "Who would they fight? The sand?"

"I found your home, Khofi. So can they."

"They are not gods. I'm not sure what they are."

"Neither gods, nor humans." Tyr observed. "They are *Didermocerus ergastor*: Trolls. They are creatures born into legend to complete a prophecy. They stood against Asgard in the final days as allies of our great enemy. And they feed upon humans when necessary. They make ready to climb toward your village, your world. What now, Khofi? Will the ants help you? Or shall I?"

"Like an ant in danger, I will hide. So will my people. The trolls will pass over us and continue on. As will we. Though I am surprised to see an army, there is no need for war. Nor—"

"Nor a god of war?" Tyr finished. "The times for armies have passed. But as you gathered your people to live as a community, to find life in peace, these remaining trolls gathered themselves in a way of life they understand. They know war and destruction."

"Perhaps they can learn peace."

"It is part of the ecology you spoke of, Khofi. Even ants have soldiers."

124

"But those soldiers do not pray to gods. Nor shall I. I still ask you to leave us, Tyr. The trolls will, too. They cannot raid what they cannot find."

"Both ants and I found you, Khofi. Though you wish me gone, I will not leave your people to the fortune of trolls or camouflage."

Tyr's metallic hand glowed. Flame flashed over the ant, and the ember of its body fell. The earth vibrated as Tyr extended his arm from the plateau's edge. An expanding wave flowed from his hand like a horizontal mirage. It coalesced into a great lens that focused sunlight beneath it. The trolls screamed as intense heat over took them. Flames erupted from the hulking creatures. The lens became blinding light, and then dissipated. The stench of charred flesh rose with the immense pall of smoke. Whatever the intention of the trolls, they were destroyed by the hand of Tyr.

"You are safe now, Khofi."

Khofi gripped his walking stick tightly and fought back the nausea from what he saw. "And what of the ant? It meant neither you nor me any harm, yet died by your hand like the trolls."

"You morn the ant? What of your people, who are now safe?"

"My people are safe, but would it have been a trouble to speak to the trolls and know their intension?"

"What is the intension of an ant? If you were a dewdrop or piece of skin, it would consume you without pity. As would the trolls."

"And you, Tyr? Would you one day forget about me as you did the ant? Such is my fear for my people. We are not an army of trolls. We are a small village. No matter. To you we are all ants."

"There is much that separates humanity from trolls, Khofi. And you from an ant."

"Yet there is little distinction between all three against your power. I can crush an ant. You can crush me, or an army.

You are a remnant of an age of escalation. But my people live in a balance with other surviving life. We must preserve that delicate order. If you wish to help us, leave the ants alone. Leave us. We will both survive, even in the face of trolls. They are hardly as fearsome as an angry god. I know. I was alive before Ragnarok."

"We did much harm. True." Tyr paused. "Yet, I am here because I stood against the cleansing fire. It could only consume me if I joined with my brothers and sisters to yield my body and be reborn. I saw our folly, our failure. I rejected our legacy. And so the pantheon will remain asleep, and Asgard in ashes. I live now to help you. Surely we can forge a bond greater than you have with the ants."

"Perhaps. I do see more in you than power alone, Tyr. It is possible time has changed your outlook. But still you are a being of power. You wield it at times without thought to the small details. And so, I stand firm. I cannot banish you, but I would never have my people rely on you. Even if you would never harm us, we need to withstand the elements on our own. If we face trolls, then they too must be overcome. Although in less spectacular ways. But if you stay, my people and our heirs will be subject to your power just as if you ruled with force. I would have them know their own power. Again, please go."

"And if I were to be unseen, known only to a few whom could call me at times of need? Is that not a sound alternative?"

Khofi drew a shallow breath. He paused to consider something he never expected. Tyr needed personal contact. Perhaps communication with other thinking people meant more than being worshiped, or to act as a protector. This god was lonely.

"I'm sorry, Tyr. Truly. The effect would be the same. Your power would be our guide, not our creativity or ability to adapt. Even now, you have thrown a delicate balance off its scale. The ants will find the bodies of the trolls and eat them. In killing the trolls, you have given us a possible plague of ants."

126

"Then I will teach you to eat ants."

Khofi sighed. "We already do. We cannot be too selective in what we consider food. In truth, we should learn to eat troll meat. It would limit the increase of ants."

"A curious solution."

"But a solution, nonetheless. Perhaps in the remains of other worlds built by Asgard, there is a place for you. But it is not here. We have finally learned to survive without your kind. We must learn to thrive this way. I see that as the future, Tyr. I bid you well. But I implore you to leave."

Tyr was silent. He looked away from Khofi and out across the desert. His face seemed close to the sky from Khofi's perspective, and it showed clear disappointment. And then a slight smile. He looked back down at Khofi.

"I was the god of war, and the god of justice as well. In that role, I alone would not yield before Sutur's flames. I shall grant your supplication, little Khofi, bravest of humanity. I shall walk the Earth, and perhaps beyond. You will not see me again, nor will my presence visit here. May your people prosper, and may the lessons taught by the folly of my kind never repeat. That is my wish for the future. I would grant you a long life, little Khofi. But it is something you already own."

Khofi eased his grip on his walking stick. The intensity of his grasp surprised him. His throbbing fingers would need time to straighten. He watched Tyr turn from him without further word and walk the narrow trail down to the desert. Khofi thought it was an unusual departure for a god. There was no soaring chariot, nor whirlwind of fire. Then again, he thought, why not be efficient.

Khofi took a deep breath. The dust stung the back of his throat. He peered over at the plateau's edge at the column of dead trolls. At night he would send a scavenging party to inspect them. One of their thick, metal spear shafts would make for a sturdy walking stick if not for the sharp, slashing points. His people, the ants, and other scavengers would harvest what they could. The desert would have the weapons. Dust stung

Khofi's eyes, but the storm was over. He felt the sun's rays searing the back of his head, and raised his hood. Despite the weather, Khofi's village would remain cool and secure within the earth. Khofi turned and walked back home. There was more work to be done before nightfall.

DISTANCE

Mark Moorehaven looked out his small window, and pondered. It might be summer. It was certainly a bright day. The strip of mown grass outside was far less glorious than past views. Yet, those memories, like so much else, were forgotten or suppressed within the folds of his mind. What never faded was a persistent and powerful longing. It was even greater than the sense of loss caused by the erosion of personal history. Mark knew he should be contemplating more than a lawn edged perfectly against the concrete walkway. These were little details. Small. Something large had once touched Mark's mind.

The landscaping was all too ordered. Mark knew life was chaotic and too vast to contain. Weeds that sprouted within the walled garden were sprayed by carefully engineered herbicides. Mark didn't tell the doctors about his longing, or that he tried to remember its origin. He feared a carefully engineered pill might erase it. Mark felt his longing was the only thing left from a life deep with memories. To regain the full truth of his life, he stayed quiet and patient. Those traits stayed with him like instincts.

Mark resolved to keep his goals hidden like that dandelion he found this morning behind the azalea. He glanced at his room's opened door. No one was looking in. He withdrew his pressed handkerchief. It held an unusual bulge. Mark wondered what was in it. He unfolded it, and smiled. He cautiously opened his window. Secretly harvested dandelion seeds wafted out of the cotton folds to drift across the level grass.

Miles away from Mark's defiance, the summer sun burned the green from unwatered lawns. Young Ryan Allen enjoyed the sun and the lessened need for the lawnmower. However, weeds flourished in his mother's garden. Running through the woods and climbing trees with his pals had to wait. To the surprise of his parents, the son who only escaped their old apartment's walls through his Play Cube's game screen loved the rustic landscape surrounding the fresh suburb cut into it. Today he crouched in the shadiest corner of the yard and began his dreaded chore.

Surface weeds gave way to a battle royal with a peculiarly large dandelion. Its leaves and flowers snapped away. Ryan growled in frustration. He dug for the root so it wouldn't sprout up again. His frustration eased. Digging was fun. He finally tore out the root and waved it triumphantly in the air like a dirty whip. Looking at his hole, the intrigue of different dirt layers inspired a deeper dig. He uncovered a slice of old streambed the housing contractor had packed with rocky fill-dirt.

Ryan's fascination with backyard geology gave way to a greater curiosity. Ryan uncovered a new root--a strange, warm root. It moved slightly when Ryan ran his hands across it. His muddy fingertips detected something like a pulse through its woody surface. Ryan figured the odd root must attach to one of the trees beyond his yard's tall, wooden fence. He dug sideways along his curious find and freed a thick nodule. The nodule turned. Ryan slowly recoiled from his small pit. A set of nearly human eyes blinked away loose earth and looked up at him.

Back inside the sterile building, most of the eyes Mark Moorehaven saw held vacant stares. All of the other patients' symptoms revealed a discernible pathology. For a lucky few there was treatment. Mark knew his condition was unique. The other patients were content with the fluorescent lighting and polished floors. They had no desire to remember life beyond the walled gardens. At times, the doctors and staff would indulge Mark's questions about them. For those rare moments, he was an equal. Then, the overworn smiles and comforting demeanor returned. Once gain Mark was no different in the staff's eyes to the blank faces perched over bathrobe cocoons in other rooms. Mark liked wearing real clothes and looking outside. There he hoped to glimpse something bigger than his current fate. Perhaps something was looking for him.

When the sprinklers ran, Mark stared at the water darkening the dry cement. He knew something more important was going on than water and hydronium trading hydrogen. His attempts to remember it would drown in small pools reflecting the sun. Close up, the mirrored sunlight blinded him from seeing the water. Mark was certain his inner blindness was as carefully maintained as the gardens. If he could step back far enough he might be able to see both the reflection and the pool.

Some distance away, Ryan had taken a step back from his new hole. At its bottom, he could see the strange eyes stare at him. They did not threaten. Instead, they held obvious curiosity about their discoverer. After several minutes of summoning bravery, Ryan cautiously brushed away the remaining dirt from the gazing nodule. When revealed, the thing attached to the root appeared to be a cross between a worm and some big bug you might find under a rock. Except for the human-like eyes. They blinked, but never looked away. More dirt fell away. More node bugs looked up. Ryan grew more confused, and excited. Six sets of eyes looked out of his pit. The first node bug never took its attention away from Ryan. He thought it looked up at him like a lonely dog wanting to make friends. Ryan shared similar thoughts about them. The idea of all six creatures as pets and the reaction of his pals thrilled him. The shouts of Ryan's mother from the kitchen startled him. It was lunchtime.

Mark Moorehaven forgot about his lunch and dinner with no remorse. Today, breakfast was a joy. As his dandelion seeds fought the chemicals, his symptoms worsened. However, he was glad to be out in the world. Mark looked at the driver as their car left the café. Civility was something he remembered. She was a nice young woman, but seemed uncertain and nervous. That was quite a contrast to the calm and assertive persona she displayed to Mark's nurses. Apparently, following restrictions, she could take Mark on brief trips. A nurse had whispered the woman's name before she entered his room.

Still, the identity of the young woman who glanced at him with strained compassion slid into the haze of his past.

"Bernie, Dad. I'm Bernie," she said. "You wanted a boy named Bernard. Bernice was as close as you got. Remember?" Bernie saw her father's pathetic grimace as struggled to do just that. She sighed. "I'm sorry."

"No. Don't be," Mark replied. "The one thing I can't forget is my memory loss. At least I realize that."

Bernie knew her father's short-term memory was weakest in the morning. He recalled things for longer in the afternoon. At least in the past. She hoped he would remember her name. It helped to reinforce the sense of ease and familiarity a person expects from close family. She felt an increasing sense of loss when quiet civility replaced that. That was present all too often in her relationship even before he went to the sterile building on the city's edge. That facility was visible in the distance as she drove passed the intersection and onto the highway. Today she took what would be the biggest risk of her life. It would be worthwhile if it only lead to a few moments to somehow reconnect with her father, alone.

"OK. I'm sorry, Bernie. I'm confused. That's where I live, right?" Mark pointed behind them.

"Yes. But we're not going back there."

"Oh?"

"We're going into the country." Bernie said.

"Okay. I'm glad. But why?"

"I wish you could tell me, Dad. This was your idea. Before you came down with the disease. It's part of a timeline."

"Timeline. I see. Timeline?"

"You planned this. You said it would take this long to grow. Whatever that means. I was to come get you today, wherever you were."

"That's very curious."

"Yes, Dad. Very."

Mark felt anticipation grow as strong as the sensation of longing. He felt in greater control the farther he traveled from his sterile room, but thought it was due more to a full stomach than distance. He began to think his patience was paying off. Then the car exited the freeway.

"Bernie, is this the way to the country?"

"No. But we need to switch cars."

"Okay. Why?"

"You said to do it in case we were followed."

"Followed? I must've been an interesting man. Once."

Bernie glanced at her father. His face was brighter. If he had been an absent parent, he was still a man to be proud of. She remembered that sentiment spoken often by her mother. Bernie held onto it and the hope that this was all worth the risk. Yet in the back of her mind was the unmistakable dread that he planned this trip during the first stage of his illness, and it was nothing more than a futile exercise of insanity. Yet, her greatest fear was that she did this as a selfish act to end her own anguish. If this trek reversed his condition, then she would never again have to visit the polished halls and suffer the eerie silence only broken by patient outbursts of madness or sorrow. She would no longer endure doctors' briefings and their new ways of saying his condition would only get worse. If his plan was a delusion, then her hopes would only be self deceit.

Still, her father's intellect was the one thing Bernie felt was unchanged. The specialists could not give her a solid diagnosis for why her father's mind selectively lost memories of his career. The symptoms grew worse after his admittance. Now his entire life experience seemed to be draining away. Maybe her father once understood what was happening to him and planned this day as a last effort to shock his memory back. Bernie hoped the barriers in his mind could be shattered and his life restored. It was quite a life. She felt those memories were worth this long drive and any silly intrigues her father had planned, and her possible arrest.

"Yeah, Dad." Bernie smiled at Mark. "You were certainly interesting. Still are."

Miles away, Ryan continued his own secret mission. Reading from a book was rare, but he needed to find support for his theory wherever he could. He slapped the encyclopedia closed, then looked to see if the noise startled anyone. His father only grumbled and continued to read his laptop's screen. Ryan was overjoyed. He had stayed home to guard his strange finds. His research was over. He concluded his node bugs were some form of cicada. Weird, giant cicadas. The fact they were wingless, attached to a root, and had human-like eyes probably meant they were some form of parasitic mutation. Mutants. That would make them even more enviable pets. He thought this might be his greatest summer, ever.

Ryan snuck outside and rearranged a thin camouflage mat of pulled weeds over the hole that hid the peering creatures. All of them now watched Ryan with a unified, constant gaze. Tomorrow he would tell his parents about them. Mom and Dad were always more agreeable to his requests during the distracting bustle before breakfast. He slipped back inside, counting the minutes until morning.

"Honey!" Ryan's father shouted to his wife while reading the news. "We're getting more neighbors."

"Oh?" Ryan's mother entered the living room. "Where?"

"That old compound north of here. It's getting bulldozed. Apartments are going up."

"Apartments!" Ryan's mother exclaimed. "Geez, Dale, we just moved away from apartments."

"Yep. Blame the developers."

"What is that place, anyway?" she asked.

"Don't know." Ryan's father answered. "It was government, or something. Some old college, I think."

Ryan almost spoke. He stopped when considering his morning goals. He kept secret that he once went inside that place. If a college was like Ryan's own grade school, then it didn't seem like a college to him. There were no desks in the rooms, but some had long tables with sinks and weird faucets. A lot of glass stuff still sat in dusty, locked cabinets. Ryan had entered the buildings through a broken window on a dare. He hadn't bargained to find company inside. Ryan remembered two men in bulky suits like wearable tents. They searched through a room and spoke through radios. Ryan made a stealthy, swift escape. His friends eventually caught up with him when he'd stopped running to catch his breath. They saw two guys with radios outside, and thought Ryan would come out in handcuffs. Ryan was pretty sure men like that didn't build apartments.

Outside in Ryan's pit, his strange discoveries sighted the stars through gaps in the dead weed camouflage. The night sky stirred urges in them from memories that were not their own. It was an emotion difficult to comprehend. Their world was the surface and soil of Earth, and their time had arrived. The pack's leader flexed its jaws preparing to move. It regarded the young target that unearthed them as a tantalizing sight, but not the prime target. Instinct and images guided the leader's decision. They would still have to transport the gift. That was their mission and reason for living. The pack was now strong enough. The leader detached itself. The pack did likewise. Together they reentered the soil and followed the growing drive to head west. In the morning, Ryan would find his pit empty. The warm root would be cold and shriveled, and the weird creatures it nurtured long departed.

The trip entered a second day. Bernie enjoyed two things. One, she had not yet been arrested. Two, driving the red compact car. It was the same model as her own car, but with AC. Mark missed the van. The seats were bigger. They took the last off ramp into their destination. A freshly painted sign welcomed them to Gatewood with bright colors. It disturbed Mark.

"This isn't right." Mark said. "Or maybe it's just different."

"Dad, do you remember this place?" Bernie had seen flashes of her father remembering things for longer. But his last comment came from long term memory. Perhaps it was because he hadn't taken his medications today. Whatever the cause, she hoped the mental barriers were breaking down.

"I think so," Mark replied as the new asphalt ramp gave way to an old, beaten roadway flanked by fallow farmland. "I think I saw this area so often there is more than one memory. Too many to block completely, maybe."

Bernie parked at a roadside store with an archaic front deck. New neon signs beamed from wood-framed windows with peeling white paint. Down the road, a new intersection cut through the old street. Traffic lights still wrapped in black plastic hung from clean, aluminum poles. Housing projects rose up from the fields beyond. Completed neighborhoods sat next to rows of unfinished frames. The construction ended against a backdrop of alders and evergreens.

"Can you remember anything from this area, Dad? You used to work somewhere around here."

"The place, maybe. Images. It was more rural then, right? I don't think they want me to recall much about the time I spent here."

"Who are they, Dad?"

"I don't think they are important now. Something else is."

"Do you know what that something is?"

"Nope."

"Do you know where to go from here?"

"Well, drive around. Not down there." Mark pointed to the new construction. "Look for older sites. Maybe something will click. We're close, Bernie. Close to something. I want to find it."

"Me, too. In the meantime, how about some coffee?"

Ryan's pit was empty. His disappointment was epic. At least he didn't tell his parents about his intended pets before checking on them. Only furrows remained where they had dug into the ground. He heard a rustling behind the wooden fence. Maybe his mutant cicadas were making a break for it in the open field. The thrill of a possible chase chilled to uncertainty and fear as Ryan reached the fence's summit. Two men in suits looked up at him. They could not appear more alien in a field of overgrown grass with scattered trees, even without waving some sort of meters. A glint of sunlight across gathering sweat lit their close clipped hair one shiny brow width above solid black sunglasses. Their knowing smiles just made them scarier. These had to be the guys his pals saw at the old buildings. The one closest to Ryan spoke.

"Hello, young man. We'd appreciate your help."

To Ryan, the man's voice had the tones of sternness and artificial friendliness a school principle used just before he calls your parents.

"Have you seen anything strange around here?" The man continued.

"Yeah," Ryan answered.

"What?" Both men asked with pointed interest.

"You guys."

"Son, we're strangers, not strange."

"I'll take your word for it. Bye." Ryan released his grip on the fence and dropped. He sprinted into his house in the split second after his feet hit the ground.

Closer than Ryan or the perspiring men in suits realized, his intended pets continued westward. The pack encountered their first obstacle. Descending a slope towards the forest, they struck compacted clay and rock where the leader expected a natural gully. It was too difficult to bore through. They had to travel over ground.

To Morton Steadholm, the sight of the pack was a shock. The little monsters erupted out of his well watered lawn as he sprayed his apple tree for aphids. The real estate agent never mentioned this area had bugs this big, this ugly, or just this flat out weird. Luckily, Morton thought, he had a weapon in hand.

The leader saw the large, rotund target approach one from the pack. Shock and fear flashed through its mind as it sprayed that one with a burning liquid. Dig! The leader ordered the pack to burrow as deep as possible. This was a threat to the mission. The leader knew it must act.

The speed of the huge bugs startled Morton. He pumped his economy size bottle of insecticide over their holes when they dove back underground. That would be the last he would ever see of them, he hoped. Sharp pain seized his left foot. Morton screamed and hopped in searing pain.

"Jenny!" he cried to his wife. "A little monster just bit me!" He dropped his weapon to clutch his foot and fell backwards. Now his whole body lay across the lawn. Adrenalin helped launch his round bulk off the grass.

"Jenny! Get the phone!" Morton cried from the safety of his concrete porch. He looked back at his lawn and feared it like open ocean during a shark attack. Today he'd call the real estate agent. Right after he dialed 9-1-1. He was definitely moving. Again.

The leader signaled his pack to resurface. He joined their swift trek over land. The member assaulted by poison grew slower. The leader knew regret, but if one became too slow or stopped the rest would have to keep moving. The mission was why they lived and must survive. It was the reason they were many, and why all members could bestow the gift alone.

At the edge of the forest, Mark and Bernie sat against the red compact just west of the houses.

"Are you sure that rundown place was where you worked, Dad? I know they shut your unit down a while ago, but that place looked really old."

"Yeah. I think so." Mark replied. "Maybe its age was part of its cover."

"Cover? Okay. But those tire tracks looked new."

"Yeah, but somehow I'm certain whatever was inside those labs is long gone. I have a feeling it's also searching for me," Mark said.

"Huh. Interesting. Are you sure this is the place?"

"Nope. I was a scientist. So with no data, I can't say I'm certain, if I ever did. I just feel we're where we should be."

"Okay. We'll hang out and see what happens."

"Say, Bernie. Do you remember what I was, what I did?"

"Yes, of course. I'm proud of you, Dad."

Mark sighed. "I'm glad. And thank you, Bernard."

"It's Bernie, Dad. It's short for—"

"I know. I'm kidding." Mark smiled broadly.

Bernie smiled. The place was quiet and shaded. Bernie sipped her cold coffee. She and her father were the only people around. The air smelled of fresh dirt and crushed pine needles. A bulldozer sat still. Its rough tracks had cut several trails into the forest. To Bernie this place looked like the start of a neighborhood park. Or a stripmall. They both looked up the slope facing them. Houses sat just beyond its crest. Bernie noticed movement in the tall grass at the base of the hill. She thought it was a squirrel or a breeze. Then she noticed her father's intent stare at the grass. The sight of what emerged made her spill her coffee.

A single member of the pack crawled with surprising speed out from the grass and straight to her father. He moved out to meet the strange thing with its human-like eyes focused on him alone. Bernie's revulsion gave way to cautious curiosity. This was weird, but maybe this thing is what her father sought. What else could it be? It was no natural creature. But what could it do for her father's mind? She stood by him and looked down at the oddity.

"Dad?"

"It's okay, Bernie. I think I know this little thing."

"How?"

"I made it. I think. Or I knew someone who did. I wish I could remember."

The pack member coiled. Bernie tensed, but Mark remained calm. A ball of clear liquid swelled from the creature's opening jaws. It waited. Mark and Bernie gasped and stared at the glistening, transparent mass. Mark haltingly moved his hands near the quivering liquid globe as if to contain it. Bernie shook out the drops of coffee from her paper cup and handed it to her father, but Mark gently tried to gather the sphere in his hands. It burst on contact and splashed over him. His skin absorbed the liquid. Mark stood, looking at his hands.

"I haven't come all this way just to—" He halted.

"Dad!" Bernie shouted as her father's eyes glazed over.

Mark smiled. "You never thought to tell me my last name, Chipper. It's not like yours."

"What?" Bernie was confused but delighted. She had her mother's last name. Her parents had never married, but remained close for her sake. She had not heard the nickname Chipper since the age of sixteen when she demanded it never be spoken again.

"It's okay, Chipper. That little thing gave me my memories. I know why they stole them from me. I wanted to tell everyone."

"Tell them what?" Bernie said in a giggle. She had been right about her father. His mind was intact all along, and now it was free of its barriers.

"I'd rather you not say what, Doctor." A man's voice intruded on Mark and Bernie's triumph. It held the tones of both sternness and artificial friendliness.

Bernie and Mark turned to see two suited men smile at them. Two more arrived in a curiously quiet black sedan.

"It would be the best for us all, Doctor." One smiling man continued.

"So says you, G-boy." Mark sneered.

"G-boy?" Bernie asked confused.

"They're too young to be a G-men, Chipper. But they're government agents. Probably N.I.B. They're the ones that stole my mind."

"As you are aware, sir, our predecessors only suppressed it." The second agent countered.

"Why?" Bernie asked. Her excitement now ebbed against a growing sense of dread.

"We don't know, ma'am." An agent in gloves with a set of clear tongs and a thick plastic sack approached them. "And we really don't want to."

Mark stood in front of Bernie as if to protect her from the pressed-suit intruders. The agent only knelt and picked up the motionless creature in front of Mark with the tongs and slid it into the plastic sack.

"No need to be dramatic, Dr. Moorehaven." The first agent said with a genuine smile. "We're not here to harm you. For you, ma'am, we have some documents we'd like you to sign."

"And if I don't?" Bernie asked defiantly.

The agent sighed. "It gets a little sticky, legally. Really, it's best just to sign. Less paperwork. Less travel time."

"Travel time?" Bernie asked. She had assumed their trip was over.

From the slope of the hill, the leader watched the others near the prime target while obscured in tall grass. The mission had been fulfilled. The nurturing vein had traveled through the soil from the point of origin and grew them outside the metal walls. Once ready, the pack set forth and delivered the gift. Yet, the leader felt the odd sensation of doubt. He signaled the other survivors. They had another journey to make.

In the night, Ryan stood outside and braved mosquitoes to stargaze. He saw countless more stars out here than at their old apartment's parking lot. Here he saw meteors, satellites, tumbling lights his dad said was space junk, and the brilliant Milky Way. Tonight, something moved in the garden. He clicked on his flashlight and aimed it at the sound. The leader and another pack member squinted in the sudden brightness.

"Yes!" Ryan shouted. He slowly approached his intended pets so they wouldn't run away again.

The leader wanted this young target to have the gift. If the prime target was unable to use it, perhaps this young one would finally enact its promise. The pack member presented the gift, knowing it would be its last act. Ryan gasped as the ball of liquid grew from the small creature's mouth. The eyes of the leader encouraged him to come closer. Ryan knelt down and shined light through the quivering globe. It was perfectly clear, like slow moving water. He nicked it with the flashlight. It burst on contact and bathed him in the liquid. Soon, images stranger than a lifetime of stargazing could give flooded his mind.

Ryan's memory was not restored like Mark's, but endowed. Mark's experience with a small group of scientists working in secrecy with materials recovered in space was strange but exciting. Yet, these memories served as a mere prelude to stranger revelations. Ryan saw an ice core slide from a metal tube. The frozen cylinder appeared to be simple ice. Melted, it seemed nothing more than water. But this water had traveled billions of miles before a sample return probe pierced a comet's heart and brought it to Earth.

"Safer and purer than from the tap." Ryan heard Mark exclaim inside his mind as past events replayed. Ryan saw Mark, against all protocols, drink a small glass of the water before all the test results were known. After his stunt, Mark knew those results would be interesting. Like Mark's mind on that day, Ryan's own became submerged in increasingly strange images. The gift was not merely Mark's memories, but also the knowledge of a mind sharing its experience across interstellar distances and a vast gulf of time.

Ancient sensation captivated Ryan's mind. He felt buoyant as if floating, and then even lighter as gravity ebbed. He was traveling at great speeds across space. The sensation was spectacular and liberating. Time slowed. Then gravity returned, only stronger. He looked back across the distance traveled. The vastness was overwhelming, but there was joy. There were voices in the distance. The promise of communication was elating. Ryan experienced memories that were either incomprehensible or their maker's own confusion. However, Ryan felt a lasting desire to try again to the bridge the vastness between suns.

Ryan felt as if he rolled in empty space and drifted into a large sphere of water impossibly liquid in the frigid darkness. A presence looked down from above the surface. Ideas permeated Ryan's mind. Water is the solvent of life. Life is the carrier of information. Information is the tool of intellect. Information was stored in the water. Ryan mentally floated inside the information and shared experience. It became part of him. He saw the water freeze and sail in the direction of the distant voices, towards whatever life might eventually find and liberate it. Information would be shared. The legacy of intellect would persist.

Ryan saw the knowledge that Mark never mentioned to anyone else. Ryan was glad it was night and that he stood outside. He stared out at the exact star where this journey started. Something far away was likely staring back, perhaps right now, hoping for a long-distance wave of hello. Once he could comprehend everything floating in his head, he'd be able to send that hello. Ryan could feel his intellect expanding. He figured this meant he would skip a few grades. Quite a few.

Mark's memories acted as a bridge between the alien knowledge and the limited experiences of a young boy. Mark had also imparted some paranoia along with the gift's knowledge. It was a wise inclusion. Not everyone was ready for this revelation and resulting revolution. And the pack, so long a carrier of the gift, had made its own contribution: urgency. These additions and the powerful longing imparted from the gift's original maker drove Ryan to his room and the Internet. His own website, cluttered with images of athletes, western outlaws, and select dinosaurs would now contain far different information. That knowledge would continuously and creatively expand across all social media and a digital universe too vast to suppress. Soon, Bernie and Mark would know their efforts finally succeeded, as would a few strange creatures living beneath Ryan's backyard. Eventually, so would other minds across a far greater depth of space, time, and memory.

ABOUT THE AUTHOR

Bruce S. Larson has seen his short stories published in several magazines, including Dark Matter, Millennium SF&F and Talebones. Bruce enjoys the sun and also the rain, although he is not a fan of being scorched or sodden wet.
WITHIN AND BEYOND: THE REALMS OF THE SUN is the second collection of his short stories.

Fans of Horror will enjoy
NIGHTMARES AND OTHER VICES, The SF-Horror Collection
Volume 1
Available for Kindle

Find more content, comments, and a blog of alternate history at Bruce's website: www.thewritebruce.com

www.ingramcontent.com/pod-product-compliance
Lightning Source LLC
Chambersburg PA
CBHW070933130626
46555CB00001B/409